The New
BLACK MASK

The New BLACK MASK

Number 5

EDITED BY

MATTHEW J. BRUCCOLI & RICHARD LAYMAN

A HARVEST/HBJ BOOK

HARCOURT BRACE JOVANOVICH, PUBLISHERS

SAN DIEGO   NEW YORK   LONDON

Editorial correspondence should be directed to the editors at Bruccoli Clark Publishers, Inc., 2006 Sumter Street, Columbia, SC 29201.

ISSN 0884-8963
ISBN 0-15-665484-9

Designed by G. B. D. Smith
Printed in the United States of America
First Harvest/HBJ edition 1986
A B C D E F G H I J

Contents

William Haggard:
An Interview

William Haggard is Richard Clayton, a former civil servant in India and London. In 1958 he published his first book, Slow Burner, *which introduced Col. Charles Russell of the British Security Executive, who has been the central figure in most of the twenty-eight Haggard thrillers. His novels pack sufficient action to be classified as page turners, but Haggard is primarily interested in character motivation and the use or abuse of responsibility. It has been remarked that his fiction provides a meeting ground for the spy story and the novel of manners—an offspring of Geoffrey Household and Jane Austen.*

He is not yet as well known in America as in England, but a reviewer in the Chicago Daily News *declared that "The most intelligent suspense novels in the English language are being written by William Haggard." An evident quality of his work is its conservative stance, which has upset liberal British critics. Nevertheless, Haggard is not primarily a political writer; he is concerned with the realities of power and the professionalism of those who exercise it.*

William Haggard is published in England by Hodder & Stoughton and in America by Walker.

New Black Mask interviewed Mr. Clayton in his home on the Essex coast.

NBM: How did you turn thriller writer?

Haggard: I was living in a place called Hartley Whitney, which is the rough equivalent of one of those little suburban New York towns, and I was com-

muting to London. On the way up I read the papers—
this was in 1958—and on the way home I read suspense novels. Now this was just before the great flood
of them. I couldn't get enough to read. I read people
like Geoffrey Household, but I didn't like Ian Fleming at all, and I thought, well possibly there's a market
here. Something between the knockabout, common or
garden-variety cliff-hanger and the later rather high-
brow, intellectual thrillers. So I had a shot at it, and
I took it to Innes Rose at the Farquharson literary
agency. He told me what seemed wrong. I hadn't constructed it properly. So I took it away. When I took
it back to him after making some changes, he said,
"You know, I can sell this to the first publisher I take
it to." And he did. He sold it to Cassell. That was the
first book I did, called *Slow Burner*. That was way
back in 1958, and I'd got rather hooked on writing
thrillers. And I went on writing thrillers.

NBM: *Slow Burner* was the first novel you ever
wrote?

Haggard: I'd never written a word before that.

NBM: No literary apprenticeship in school? Writing for the school magazines? That sort of thing?

Haggard: I wrote the house notes for my school,
but that's the lot. I'd never written anything else. Or
ever thought of writing fiction. It must be in the blood,
because my mother's name was Haggard. That's why
I took it. As you know, there was a very successful
Victorian writer called H. Rider Haggard, but I'm not
descended from him. My grandfather wrote a lot of
pamphlets, so I suppose the itch to write was in the

2

blood. So there it was. I took this up, and it seemed to go very well. One thing that went very strongly for me was that I'd read a lot of American authors.

NBM: Which ones?

Haggard: Ones that you've probably never heard of. People like Joseph Hergesheimer and Willa Cather, twenties and thirties. Now at that time my own contemporaries were swooning over Aldous Huxley or Rosamund Lehmann and that sort of thing. I couldn't stomach it. I had to read some sort of fiction when I was an undergraduate. Undergraduates did have time to read fiction in the twenties. So I read these people. I still have an almost complete collection of Hergesheimer, which I very much treasure. I think he's a much-underestimated novelist. The only other man I know of who shared that opinion is the American critic H. L. Mencken. He thought a lot of him. Well, I share his view. I think he was superb at it.

NBM: Your work is nothing like Hergesheimer's. His writing is lush.

Haggard: Very lush. Mine's very spare. I've been told I have difficulty getting it up to sixty or seventy thousand words—have to pad it a bit sometimes. My natural length is about fifty thousand words, and of course no publisher wants that.

NBM: Beyond the fact that you enjoyed reading them, why, when you commenced writing, did you settle on the intrigue or espionage novel rather than the murder novel?

Haggard: Two reasons. First, I had a political background in which I was a civil servant. I started life as a civil servant in India. Then in the war I was in the Indian army, and I went to the Staff College; and after I came out of it I went into—not the Intelligence Corps—but a department which ran the business of operating the Funnies. You know, finding them boots and stopping them sending telegrams to the viceroy. That sort of thing. So I had that background. Also, to a certain extent I enjoyed using the books as vehicles for my own political background. Which indeed I'm afraid they are.

NBM: They certainly are, and some of the English reviewers are really irritated by them.

Haggard: They don't like it a little bit. There's one of them writes those infuriated reviews in the *Glasgow Herald*—also in the *New Statesman,* needless to say.

NBM: It seems to me that you're saying something about the decline of English character, about the decline of the English sense of responsibility and duty. I read your works as a lament for the English standards that have vanished since World War II.

Haggard: I agree with that. They *are* laments. Also I once had to put it this way: I don't think myself that the real enemy is communism. I think it's liberal humanism. That's what we call it. The wet Left. And to my mind it's the wet Left that's bringing us down. We may one day indeed even need communism to brace us up again.

NBM: Because they at least have discipline?

Haggard: They at least have discipline—and how. I was born in a country vicarage, where it's very simple. We weren't poor, but we were very far from rich.

4

And that makes you extremely competitive. You can always tell children of the vicarage. People like Virginia Wade. You couldn't get anything more competitive than Virginia Wade. You see, the background was: Look! you're just as good as the boys up at the big house. Just as good. We can give you a good education, and after that you're on your own. We can't leave you any money. We'll send you to a good school and university if you can get in—which in those days wasn't that difficult—and then you're on your own.

I went to Lancing, and then I went to Oxford—Christ Church. And then I went into the Indian civil service. And during the war, since I had a reserve commission, I went into the Indian army. I got mixed up in intelligence there. I don't say I was concerned with intelligence gathering at all, evaluating it. I wasn't. But I was certainly very concerned with keeping it on its feet. And preventing it doing anything too outrageous, because intelligence officers are very strange people. I mean they do very unmilitary things. They're apt to be extroverts. And then when I came back I went to the home civil service. I then got mixed up in something called Enemy Property, of which I became controller in time. And in 1957 I realized that I hadn't got that much more time to do in the Civil Service—this was another factor in my turning to writing. I would have an adequate pension, and by that time I had made a little money. But what was I going to *do*? How was I going to fill the day? So I thought, well, I'll try my hand at writing, and I did. And I stayed with Cassell's until they blew up. I was very happy with Cassell's. As you know, they were bought by another publisher that didn't do any fiction at all. Then I went to Hodder & Stoughton where I'm even more happy. I've always had very happy relationships with my publishers. I've always got on with them.

NBM: For a while Penguin did a splendid job with you. Back in the sixties, Penguin had you in every railroad station newsstand in England. But you're not published by Penguin now.

Haggard: It was my publishers who sold the secondary rights. They told my agents that they'd sell them to so and so. Later they sold them to some others, but at the moment I haven't got a paperback publisher in England. I've got three unpublished novels in America, which I'm not too worried about. What I am worried about is the past. I don't feel that I've been given an entirely fair crack of the whip. Walker took me gladly enough in America, and I don't think they lost money on me, after the Detective Book Club and after paperbacks and so on.

NBM: I'll put it this way: much less interesting writers are doing much better in America. Americans are being deprived of splendid reading. The kind of novel that you write isn't written by anyone else I know.

Haggard: Certainly not Len Deighton and certainly not le Carré.

NBM: It's Haggard. I think Americans will respond to Colonel Russell because Americans are hero worshipers, and Colonel Russell obviously represents, for you, the best in English character.

Haggard: Yes, yes. Even I regard him as a slight hero.

NBM: But let's take a closer look at just what Russell represents. We've already said standards: courage, honor, duty, responsibility. Those things that were once thought of as the cornerstones of English character. Beyond expressing your respect for these things, are you also issuing warnings? Are you telling your readers, "Look—"

Haggard: Unless we get back to these, we shall need the Russians in to put us straight. But we are collapsing now. I'm convinced of this. It doesn't matter which government you've got, but under our present constitutional system, or under any government we're likely to have, we're going to sink to the level of Malta.

NBM: When did it start? Did it start post World War II or did it start with the intellectuals of the thirties?

Haggard: I reckon what broke us was the First World War, because that took the finest of our young lives and it cost us a terrible lot of money. Germany has beaten us twice, really. It has indeed. Look at Germany now, it's stinking rich. Now you ask me, "Are you sounding a warning?" Perhaps I am, but not deliberately. I'm not a Billy Graham about it.

NBM: But it's there.

Haggard: But it's there. Oh yes, I have to admit

that. For instance, that reviewer that I've been talking about: when he wants to be nasty about Russell he calls him a Boy Scout, which is slang for being a bit of a goodie, a bit overkeen. Well, different, having old-fashioned values, like discipline and keeping your nose clean.

NBM: This list of your titles takes us up to '84, and it's over twenty-five novels. How long does it take you to write a novel?

Haggard: I take much more time getting the framework up, the steelwork up, than I do writing the book. I'm not one of those writers who says, "I'm going to start a book today," and goes out and buys a quire of paper and starts writing. I can't do it that way. You must have a firm plot, and you must have enough incident in it—not necessarily recurring at regular intervals. All of this sounds terribly corny, but it is in fact how thrillers are constructed.

NBM: Do you have a full outline when you start?

Haggard: I have a chapter outline as to what happens for, say, fifteen chapters, the main occurrences, playing the dialogue against the description, and so on. All the old tricks. All the old corny tricks. But that takes me much longer than actually writing the book, which I can do in—well, given a fair run, I can do it in twelve weeks, comfortably. The actual writing and then typing out.

NBM: Longhand first?
Haggard: Oh, yes.
NBM: And then typescript?
Haggard: Yes.

NBM: Do you do your own typescript, or send it out to a secretary?

Haggard: No, I do my own. But only because only I can read my handwriting.

NBM: Morning writer?

Haggard: I write in the morning. I get up early, write for two or three hours, then go shopping, and then my friend and I have lunch. And then—a habit I acquired in the East—I have a couple of hours sleep in the afternoon. And then start the day again.

NBM: Russell's age is a bit of a problem, isn't it? You got him to about sixty, and in the recent novels he seems rather younger.

Haggard: In the last two novels; he only appears as a reference character. Now I had to talk this out with my publishers and my agents. He'd been replaced by a very anglicized West Indian, which I'm told went quite successfully. This chap went to Harrow and has become very English. And he has a delightful wife.

I had to talk to my publishers about replacing Russell, because they said you can't really get away with Russell forever. They all said that I rather tended to project myself into Russell. To a certain extent he *was* what I would rather like to be, if I'd been a regular soldier, if I'd been Anglo-Irish, and if I'd been in the Irish Guards. But he's got a lot of other characteristics. And they said, "Well, you simply can't get away with this. He's too old. He can't be jumping out of windows and doing the things he does. You've just got to have a younger protagonist." So I thought up this West Indian.

9

NBM: Let's return to the wet Left, please.

Haggard: I can't tell you much about the Left except I don't like them.

NBM: I mean in terms of what they have done to English society. When did it begin, in the thirties?

Haggard: I reckon early thirties or very late twenties. I came out of the University in 1929. It wasn't noticeable then. I went to India in 1932 when it was just noticeable. I came back in 1936 and got married. And then it was very noticeable. The sheer decay of standards. I realize I'm simply an old fogy. And the books show it. But I'm not going to change at my age. I'm pretty much dyed-in-the-wool by now.

NBM: Is it accurate to say that these Left intellectuals are motivated by a curious self-hatred?

Haggard: Entirely. Self-hatred, and another factor, particularly with the rich ones, guilt. What do they do about it? Nothing. Do they give their money away? No sir. They do not give their money away. They keep it. They run big houses. They're all as bogus as a three-dollar bill. I've met them when I was working in London. But one thing I've always kept away from is literary society. I never went to publishers' parties or mixed with the Left writers. Never. Even when I was actually living in London myself, in Doctorland near Harley Street. But I got a very strong distaste for them, a sort of instinctive mistrust. It's just like I didn't like rats.

NBM: One of the things that reviewers seem to complain about is your insistence that there are racial characteristics, there are racial differences.

Haggard: That is taboo thinking.

NBM: It seems very clear in your novels, for example, that most Indians are not to be trusted. And you prefer Turks to Greeks.

Haggard: I much prefer Turks to Greeks. I don't like Greeks. So far as the Indian martial races are concerned, I have great admiration for them: Sikhs, Marathas, Gurkhas. They're mostly yeoman peasant stock: the eldest son runs the land, and the youngest son goes into the army. Just like that. They've done it for generations. I have the greatest respect for them. But apart from them, the rest of India is a four-letter word.

NBM: You regard the Swiss and the French as both feckless and bribable.

Haggard: Infinitely bribable. The French are merely a nuisance. They've never forgiven the Anglo-Saxons for saving them. I don't like Germans, but I greatly admire them. In fact, you'll get a bottle of German wine for lunch.

NBM: Do you read detective fiction?

Haggard: The standard detective novel, what they call the cozies—Agatha Christie—I can't read. And I cannot read what we call the "whydunits."

NBM: Who are the authors of the "whydunits"?

Haggard: Julian Symons. People like that. The genre starts off by having a crime, tells you on the first page who's done it, and spends the rest of it in amateur psychology, explaining he didn't get on with his wife. If I want to read psychology, I want to read the hard stuff that tells you what it's really about or what a good priest will tell you. They're all laid in some dreary south London suburb. Some little man going into London every day on the bus throttles his wife because she won't sleep with him or something. The thing becomes excruciatingly boring. They're not crime stories at all. There's no crisis, there's no solution, there's nothing. It just carries you through this chap's mind and his relations with his wife, or his mistress, or his girl friend, or whatever. They're all sex murders in one way or another. And I find them intensely boring. Of the current thrillers, I think Len Deighton's good. I can't read le Carré.

NBM: Why not?

Haggard: There's too much *angst* in it. He's an angry young man, or angry old man.

NBM: What's he angry about?

Haggard: The world. And that's too large a target. The way the world is run. He's angry with the whole system. And it doesn't do. Well, I'm angry with it too, but I've got to live with it. He appears to think he can change it. I know he can't.

NBM: But his George Smiley is not all that far from Colonel Russell. Same kind of man, old-fashioned standards, doing the job, getting on with it, and battling the incompetents and frauds in the government.

Haggard: That is in fact what does happen.

NBM: If Colonel Russell really had power, if he were, say, a senior minister, what would he do?

Haggard: I must slip that one, because I can't conceive him as a politician, at least not one under the democratic system. I mean, he might, just conceivably, start some—I hate the word fascist—organization, but I can't see him working as a politician. In fact, I've always been rather careful to draw the distinction between what he does and what he's told to do, which is noticeable in several books when he bends the law at risk of his own head. But fortunately he gets away with it.

NBM: He doesn't need the job, which helps.

Haggard: He doesn't need it, no. He's a man in comfortable financial circumstances, and therefore he's prepared to take a chance and does. But I can't see him as a politician. I don't know what he'd do. I just can't see him taking it on. I think he'd go mad. I'm sorry I can't answer that. I've never even thought what he'd do. I certainly wouldn't ever consider a book in which he was in a political job. Never. No, it's not his cup of tea at all.

NBM: But you think it is at least conceivable that, given the proper inducements, he could join an extra-governmental political movement.

Haggard: Put it this way; I'm sure if Russia successfully invaded this country tomorrow, the first man they would employ would be Colonel Russell.

NBM: And he'd work for them?

Haggard: Oh yes.

NBM: Why?

Haggard: Discipline. The first people they'd shoot would be the intellectual Left. They're all going to concentration camps, or, if they're lucky, going to be shot. But people like Russell . . . The hard Right has got much more in common with communism than the soft Left.

NBM: Colonel Russell and the class system or William Haggard and the class system. You uphold it?

Haggard: Oh yes, uphold it strongly, but I'm not a snob. I know which class I was born to.

NBM: Define *snob* for me.

Haggard: That's asking something. Now in the old days it used to mean "climber," roughly a man who sought the company of, or kowtowed to, those in a class above him. Now it appears to mean, as currently used, anybody who dares to admit that class exists. I know exactly what class I belong to. I belong to what we used to call the professional upper-middle class. I have no wish to be anything else. I'm not upper class and never shall be.

NBM: But the Colonel is, isn't he?

Haggard: The Colonel, I suppose, is. Yes. He's upper class, but I hope he's not offensively so.

NBM: Would you say that the English upper class have betrayed their responsibilities?

Haggard: Not betrayed them, they've failed them. There was no act of deliberate betrayal, I'm sure.

NBM: Failure of character?

Haggard: There's no drive, I think. After all, there's a lot to be said for them. If you're inbred as they are you can't have particularly powerful genes. If you line-breed a dog . . . There's a very common dog around here, hunt terriers—some people call them Jack Russells, but they're not—and they are linebred until they become absolutely daft.

The upper class has been clipped of a good deal of power deliberately. The House of Lords now has no power at all. It's a sort of old boys' club. And all these life peers have been pumped into it because it's a cheap way of pensioning off politicians. Because they get paid to attend, whereas proper peers don't. It's got no power over a money bill. It can hold up and it can send a bill back through the Commons. But if the Speaker of the House of Commons certifies the thing as a money bill, House of Lords can't effectively touch it.

NBM: Would it be accurate to say that one of the things Colonel Russell does is uphold the class system?

Haggard: No. I don't think it would. I'll put it this way: He's aware of it but has long since given up hope of changing the direction of the world. He mistrusts what the sillies call egalitarianism, which doesn't mean a thing. I don't think he's conscious of his class at all; in fact it's one of the nice things about him. He just is upper class and that's all, as the nicer ones are. I went to a college at Oxford which was full of the upper class, and I wasn't treated any different because I wasn't.

NBM: Why should Americans read you? What will they get from your work?

Haggard: I suppose something about the decadent limey state. Because I do feel we are decadent. I may not be, but then I'm old. I'm finished.

NBM: Could it be that your work requires a greater knowledge of English society than American readers have?

Haggard: Yes. I like that question; I think you put your finger on it. Certainly a greater knowledge than the average inhabitant of Croaking Bull, Ohio, has. I don't imagine that I would play in Peoria. So I can't imagine Haggard being read in Peoria. Why should they? It isn't all that exciting; it certainly isn't notably sexy.

NBM: I'm sure that someone along the line has said to you, "Look, if you really want to sell your books, you have to put in some bedroom scenes." What was your response?

Haggard: I may have been in a bedroom myself, but that doesn't make me a good writer of bedroom fiction. Those blow-by-blow accounts of sexual intercourse bore me stiff. That's something you do, not something you write about. What's that chap called who writes bloody great blockbusters full of sex? Harold Robbins. I can't read Harold Robbins, can you?

NBM: Why does le Carré sell in Peoria? Not because of sexual content.

Haggard: I can't answer that. Well, he has a certain air of *gravitas*, which I haven't. He's much more solemn than I am. That's why I find him rather a difficult read. I don't share his view of life. He has the extreme Protestant ethic—that what counts is that you have to find your own way to God.

NBM: Why has the spy novel become such a popular genre? In the old days there were E. Phillips Oppenheim and John Buchan and almost nobody else. Is it all response to the conditions of the cold war?

Haggard: Yes. But I wouldn't call Fleming a spy writer. In fact, he writes adventure stories. I can see why they're madly popular and made into marvelous films, because something happens every second. They are action-packed; the action is the story.

NBM: In his early novels I think he was trying to say something serious about terrorism. It seems to me that Fleming was the first novelist to recognize terrorism as a subject for fiction.

Haggard: Yes. I've just turned in a book to Hodder & Stoughton called *The Martello Tower*, written about this coast, about terrorism. It will be out next year. It's based on the idea that this coast is riddled with mud creeks, and they're all guarded by those Martello Towers which we put up against Napoleon. And smuggling still goes on, but it's soft smuggling. Things like silk, brandy, and perfume. What happens in this book is what happens if a terrorist takes it over, starts bringing in arms and mortars.

NBM: To what purpose?

Haggard: Attacking the royal family when they're on a state drive. You could put a mortar two miles away. That's two thousand meters. It's quite a range. You can put that mortar anywhere, but you can't control the whole of London with police. You put it somewhere in a backyard in Tottenham or somewhere like that. They're very accurate. You can land them on a blanket. Imagine a royal procession going up the Mall with a couple of mortars firing. If you've got a good crew, you can get up to fifteen rounds a minute. The Mall would be a holocaust. Fifteen rounds a minute. If you've got two mortars, thirty a minute. You're going to hit something. You might not hit the royal coach, but you'll wipe out the bodyguard and everything else and the spectators. So that's quite a story.

NBM: What do you hope that your canon amounts to?

Haggard: I don't grade it higher than high-class entertainment. I'm not a message writer. If you're asking me have I got any message to give a suffering world, the answer is emphatically no. If it can give intelligent people some amusement, I'm satisfied. I'm afraid I am writing for people of above-average intelligence, because I just can't read pulp, so why should I write it? No, I am an entertainer basically. I've no serious message. I don't try to convert anybody to anything. I'm a complete skeptic myself. I look at every statement. I don't take it on trust. You've got to have a bloody good look at it yourself.

NBM: The celebrated mythical reader: who do you see as your ideal reader?

Haggard: In America I haven't an idea. In this country I have a pretty shrewd one. It's somebody over forty or even over forty-five. I don't think I appeal to the young very much. Somebody who would rather read a civilized book than goggle the box. Somebody of a certain standard of education, not necessarily Yale or Oxford. Somebody who can appreciate a writer who doesn't take too many chances with the English language—which I don't. I take a lot of chances with syntax but none with grammar, absolutely none. Somebody who realizes the subjunctive tense still exists; somebody who appreciates it when you say "whatsoever it be" rather than "whatsoever it is." In other words, a fairly educated reader.

NBM: You used the word *civilized* a moment ago. What is a "civilized reader"?

Haggard: A civilized reader is a reader with a certain standard of education.

NBM: The genre you write in is perceived as a mass genre, a popular genre.

Haggard: Oh yes. The spy story or the suspense novel. That is perceived to be a mass genre. Oh yes, I would agree with you. But I wouldn't agree that everybody writing in that genre has to aim at a mass readership. I certainly don't.

NBM: If you were starting over, if it were 1958 again and you were turning novelist at the improbable age of fifty-one, with what you have learned from your thirty books, what changes would you make in your career plan?

Haggard: None.

NBM: You've written what you wanted to write?

Haggard: Yes, I've written what I wanted to write, and the only thing I'm capable of writing. I could never sit down and write one of what they call "sensitive" novels, that sort of delicate interplay where nothing happens. P. G. Wodehouse once described it beautifully as one of those books in which little happens for eighty thousand words and on the last page the undergraduate decides not to commit suicide after all. That sort of book I had no ambition and no sort of gift to write.

Timeo Danaos

WILLIAM HAGGARD

*William Haggard has written few short stories,
preferring the space of the novel, which allows him
to develop his plots. He regards "Timeo Danaos"
as his most successful story. It first appeared in
Winter's Crimes 8 (London: Macmillan, 1976);
this is its first publication in America.*

AGNES WITHERS, who'd been born van der
Bijl, could do most things but blindly follow
convention. She realised that on this island she'd asked
for it, since she'd flown in the face of the local estab-
lishments. The English here were traditionally pro-
Greek, accepting the prevalent view of the Turks as a
barbarous and inferior people. Agnes Withers was
therefore odd girl out. Poets had sung of the Isles of

Greece, politicians of democracy's cradle. Agnes cared not a fig for either. Northern Dutch by birth and now British by marriage, she had a simple and often alarming directness which a Greek would most surely mistake for stupidity, and a disinclination to hide her opinions which were as Dutch as the *Rubensplein*, Dutcher than Bols. She thought that the Turks had been fiddled and diddled, despised in what was still partly their country as a helot and uncivilised people. That couldn't go on forever, of course: they were bound to come in and take what belonged to them. Once it had almost happened already, and Agnes looked forward to when it did. Since she never concealed her views from anyone, it was natural that all Greeks detested her.

And now she'd been called to the local police station, and the signature was clearly Greek. To one who could read the island's omens that signature was coldly ominous, for this wasn't a formal no-go area where a Greek policeman would have been run out of town, but an oasis of comparative tolerance where the two races lived as near to peace as events in the rest of the island let them. But now they had changed the head man to a Greek. "Inspector," he'd written below his name, which could only mean they were tightening up. The last one had been a Turkish sergeant. Agnes had called him *Çavus Bey*, which wasn't quite correct and she knew it, but it had amused him and also flattered him greatly. She had learnt to speak Turkish and spoke it well. She wouldn't or couldn't speak Greek at all.

Another black mark, she thought, unrepentant, as she put on an ancient linen hat. Normally she never wore one. Well, she'd better go up to the station and see.

She began to walk steadily up the hill, a striking woman in the prime of her life. She went at a brisk light infantry pace, since she'd a pound or two to lose and meant to. Above her was the little town from which this troublesome Inspector had summoned her, and above that again was the underground lake without which these smiling fertile slopes would be as dourly parched, as grimly impoverished, as the land on the other side of the mountain. Below her the ground fell away to the sea, a warm blue sea in the strong spring sunshine.

She had gone perhaps three hundred yards when the gunman pulled his trigger and got her. He'd been hidden behind a wall and fired quickly. Agnes Withers fell down in the dark red dust.

She lay there for at least five minutes, for the busy road had emptied magically. One minute it had been full of people, carts, and the occasional lorry; the next the dust on which she lay could have been sand in an uninhabited desert. This island had heard plenty of gunfire and had developed its own technique to deal with it: you simply hadn't been there at the time.

Agnes Withers lay still and considered calmly, for she realised she hadn't been seriously wounded. From its blast, the weapon had been a shotgun, and its owner had been less than a marksman. Just the same, her left leg was decidedly painful and it was probable she couldn't use it. So she lay till she saw the old man, walking strongly.

"Zekky," she called. "Come here and help me." Zekky was a Turk and her gardener. He lived with an unmarried daughter, and this daughter was Agnes's general maid. She wouldn't have Greek servants inside her house.

He'd been too far away to hear the shot and was also a little dim in the head; he hadn't noticed that the road was deserted, but he could see a woman lying prone in it. He broke into a lumbering canter.

When he arrived at his mistress he wished her good morning, then stood over her and thought it out. It took him some time to do so; he was slow. Finally he asked, "You are ill?"

She almost said, "I've been shot," but didn't. Instead she told him, "I've hurt my leg." He might or might not notice the wound. He was getting pretty blind by now and there didn't seem to be much blood.

"You would wish to go home?"

"Do you think you could carry me?"

The old man didn't bother to answer. He bent his strong back and picked her up. He didn't sling her across his shoulder but carried her, three hundred yards down the hill to her villa. His daughter, the maid, was already there and together they put Agnes to bed. The maid saw the wound and began to clamour. Agnes silenced her at once.

"It is nothing."

"But your ladyship has been shot. The police . . ."

"Keep away from the police."

She understood that without asking questions.

"But go and get the doctor quickly."

The doctor arrived on his moped in half an hour. He was a Belgian struck off the Belgian Register, and he wasn't supposed to practise at all. But "practise" was an elastic word, and there were more ways of paying a man than with money. The authorities knew most things about him but had shrugged their shoulders in resignation. He wasn't taking much bread from local leeches, for however pro-Greek were the British in theory, they preferred a doctor from nearer home. They were that sort of people with that sort of prejudice. So this doctor made a modest competence provided he didn't flaunt that he did so, and any Englishman needing serious surgery could mostly afford to fly home to receive it.

He looked at Agnes's leg and whistled. "Gunshot wound," he said with professional blandness; he looked again, then added softly, "Just between the two of us. You call the tune."

Like Agnes's maid he knew local form.

"Naturally," she said in Dutch. The doctor had learnt a good deal of English, but she could understand Flemish and he her Dutch.

"It isn't very serious, but I'll have to give you a local injection."

She knew that he wasn't supposed to do it. There was nothing to prevent him prescribing—there was nothing to stop any oaf prescribing if a second was fool enough to accept it—but using a hypodermic was near the line "Thank you," she said. Agnes Withers meant it.

He took out the pellets and looked at them quizzically. "Number eight shot, I think," he said. "What they use for the birds."

"I'm not a bird."

The doctor had bandaged her up and laughed. For a Fleming he had a sharp sense of humour. "Since you offer the opening, no, you are not. But I can see that the Greeks might well think you a pest. Your political opinions, you know—"

"They've reached your ears?"

"They could hardly fail to. If I may say so, you're a very Dutch Dutchwoman."

"Eoka?" she asked softly.

He shrugged. "I'm inclined to discount it and pretty strongly. Eoka is away in the mountains, and in any case whoever shot you was hardly up to their standard of marksmanship." He considered, then added blandly again, "Have you offended anyone recently? I mean rather more than you always do. More than just disliking them and not bothering to hide your contempt."

"It's as bad as that?"

"I'm afraid it is."

"Well, I knocked a man about a bit."

"You did *what?*" He was shaken.

"He was only a youth, but he'd busted the greenhouse. I'm trying to grow some English roses, and when my husband comes down for visits here he experiments with sprays and powders for an answer to the local greenfly. When I found this youth he'd smashed most of the glass, and when he saw me he picked up a pot and threw it. It didn't hurt much, but I lost my temper. There was a pickhelve around, so—"

"Say nothing more, please." The doctor sighed. A woman beating a man—unforgivable. Unforgivable down to the grave and beyond it. He asked at last, "Did you tell the police?"

"Of course I didn't."

"And not of this wound?"

"That's rather more tricky. I was on my way to see the police when whoever it was took a pretty poor shot at me. Since they'd sent for me, not vice versa, they're pretty sure to come here when I don't turn up."

"Tricky, as you say."

"But manageable. I shall tell them I've sprained my ankle badly. They're hardly likely to pull the sheets down. Old Zekky is too far gone to remember even if he ever noticed, and his daughter won't talk to a Greek on principle."

"But I thought the local boss was a Turk?"

"He was, but they've changed him."

"I don't like that. For God's sake, be careful."

"I've lived here for nearly six years. I'll survive."

The doctor rose and took his leave. He thought Lady Withers excessively tactless, but he admired her forthrightness and envied her courage. Just the same, she had used the word *survive*. He very sincerely hoped she would, but if they had really marked her down . . .

He shrugged again. There was nothing he could do about that in this race-torn, corrupt, and bloodstained island.

The new Inspector arrived on the doctor's heels. The maid showed him in, and he bowed and sat down. Agnes saw what she'd expected to see, a slick town Greek in a carefully pressed uniform. He had crisp, curly hair, not too clean but pomaded, with a pencil moustache over rather coarse lips. He wore dark glasses which were quite unnecessary. The Inspector saw an attractive woman with startlingly blue eyes and still naturally blonde hair. He put her in her later twenties. In fact, she was a little more.

"My name is Zephos," he said. "Inspector."

"It is kind of you to call here."

"Not at all. It has reached me that you met with an accident as you were presumably on your way to see me."

He left it at that, for the next move was hers. As it happened, he had the whole story on ice, for he knew she had clobbered a petty thief, and a youth had been seen with a gun and reported. The trouble about that simple equation was that the boy's uncle was a politician, neck-deep in the island's least savoury scandals. The Inspector could never book this boy, his job wouldn't last a week if he did, and he was a good deal more than a simple policeman. But if Agnes complained, he must go through the motions of trying to hunt her assailant down. That, though a fiddle and therefore congenial, would also be a tedious business, and like most Greeks he was very easily bored. But equally she had motive for silence. He had an even chance that she wouldn't embarrass him.

So he was relieved when she simply repeated, "An accident. I was clumsy and tripped. I've sprained my ankle."

"I trust it will be well in a fortnight."

Most women might well have reacted obliquely, but Agnes asked promptly, "Why a fortnight?"

"Because that is all the time you have left. After that I'm afraid you must leave this island."

For once she thought before she spoke. So she'd been right to think they were tightening up, that the change from a Turk to a slick Greek policeman was an omen of worse things to come. With the water from the underground lake, these slopes were fertile, their inhabitants prosperous, and Turks held good land as well as Greeks. But any Turk with good land was always vulnerable: they caught his land with some crooked lawsuit or maybe he simply lost his water rights. Without water his fields would be useless in weeks.

Silently Agnes Withers swore. She saw world politics with exemplary realism. In the American Congress there was a powerful Greek lobby, but there wasn't a soul to speak for poor Turks.

But this time she answered almost mildly. "You intend to withdraw my permit of residence?"

"I regret the decision, but I have my instructions."

It was a lie, for he was a natural bully. In any case he detested this woman. Beating up boys and speaking good Turkish, refusing to employ Greek servants, shooting her mouth about local rackets. His bile rose, but he kept his temper.

So, with a secret struggle, did Agnes; she asked mildly again, "May I know the reason?"

"I don't see why I shouldn't tell you. It would have to come out in any case if you were foolish enough to complain to your diplomats." He looked at her. "May I smoke?"

"If you must."

He lit a cigarette, black and noxious, and Agnes, who loathed tobacco smoke, drew away as far as the bed allowed. Her room was going to stink for a week.

"We have evidence you're a Turkish agent."

"*Godverdomme*," Agnes said instinctively.

"You consider that opinion extravagant? Then please listen to a little story." Now his voice had an edge; he was greatly enjoying himself. "Four days ago Turkish fighters flew over here, an outrageous breach of our sovereign airspace. Over this village they dipped and came low."

"They weren't saluting me."

"That is probable. They were reading the message you'd put out on your lawn."

She knew this was ridiculous, but all Greeks were suspicious, psychopathically edgy, and the charge had a sort of crazy logic. For four days ago had been a Monday, and on Mondays the maid washed the sheets and pillow slips. Being Turkish, she didn't hang them on lines; she pegged them out on the lawn to dry in the sun.

Agnes knew it was futile to argue with policemen, but silence could be read as admission. "I can only assure you that you're quite mistaken."

He didn't answer her but rose instead; he walked to the window, threw his stub into the garden, and when he returned he was openly menacing.

"I do hope you'll think it over carefully. Your house will be sold if you haven't done so and the proceeds remitted freely to England. Your furniture will follow. Consider it. You haven't, if I may say so, madam, the reputation of a tactful woman, but surely for once discretion is indicated. A discreet disappearance back to England."

He walked to the door and saluted respectably. "Think it over," he said. He went away.

Agnes sent for the maid, and she wheeled the bed out to the sunny veranda. The lawn was covered with linen again, and Friday wasn't a day for washing. The maid saw her puzzled frown and explained.

"There was too much on Monday to do in one go, so I finished the leftovers early this morning."

"Thank you," Agnes said. She slept.

She woke from her sleep to the roar of aircraft. They were flying very low again, right over her house in a tight goose V. She could see the star-and-crescent markings.

There was a telephone by her bed and she reached for it, but her hand was still in the air when it rang.

"Lady Withers?"

"Speaking."

"I see that you do not heed fair warning. I thought it generous to have given a fortnight. Regretfully it is now a week. A week to return to your husband in England." Like most Greeks, he'd assumed since they lived apart that they weren't on good terms and had more or less parted. The opposite was in fact the truth.

"Inspector . . ." Agnes began.

No answer.

She put the receiver down and then dialed, an immediate call to England, to Wiltshire. It came through in an hour, but not Sir William. He was the boss, and it took time to find him. When he was found he said casually, "Nice to hear from you."

"I don't think you're going to think so."

"No?"

"I'm in serious trouble."

"You do not surprise me."

"Can you come down here at once?"

"Of course."

There hadn't been even a second of doubt, no talk of his work or important engagements. She knew he had many; she loved him dearly. His voice went on without hint of resentment.

"I'll get a seat on the overnight flight this evening. Just meet me at the airport, will you?"

"I've been shot in the leg."

"Then get a taxi."

She met him at five o'clock the next morning, having ordered a car with a Turkish driver. This was partly because she favoured Turks, but also for a more practical reason: with a Turk she could drive to the airport directly, through the no-go land where all Greeks went in convoy. The other way round the hills was much longer.

She eagerly watched him come down the gangway, a spare man in his fifties, not showing his age. It had been a rum sort of marriage, she thought, but successful. He had married her because he'd had to. They had met at a party, and both had been tight. Three weeks later she had known she was pregnant. Distinctly un-Dutch, but she'd also been younger.

He hadn't been Sir William then, and her own family had been influential. She knew that he'd always been quietly ambitious and her family, if they couldn't break him, could put his career back by many years. They'd held the gun; William Withers had bowed to it.

She smiled as she remembered it. How Willie had carried the whole thing off! He'd arrived in Amsterdam in style, with a Bentley which he'd happened to own and a manservant whom he'd temporarily hired, where he'd put up in a suite in the Doelen Hotel. He could afford all three since he was comfortably off. Then he'd telephoned to her father politely. The marriage, he understood, was at noon so he'd arrive at the church at a quarter to. Yes, he'd be suitably dressed and attended. He'd remembered to bring a best man.

He'd rung off.

Lady Withers laughed, for she still thought it funny. To a shotgun wedding you took your Purdey, not some miserable pumpgun made in Belgium.

Then he'd driven her off on a formal honeymoon, and on it she had fallen in love with him. Not that that had solved all problems. Her baby had, alas, been born dead, and they'd told her she couldn't have another. And she hadn't liked England, or not darkest Wiltshire. They'd had a comfortable house in the guarded Establishment, but Establishment life she had found intolerable, the endless jockeying and the bitchy women. It had been Willie himself who in the end had suggested it. Why didn't she go and live on that island, the island where they'd spent most of their honeymoon? He'd have his work, which she knew absorbed him, and he'd visit her every six weeks at most. That is, if she wished it.

She'd said she did. The Inspector of Police had been ludicrously wrong. Their married life was a series of honeymoons.

So she watched him come down the gangway eagerly. He was twenty years older than she was—what of it? He knew precisely what he was doing and did it. She wouldn't change him for any debutante's dream.

He went through customs and came up to the car. "Kind of you to meet me," he said. It was typical Sir William Withers, and Agnes had accepted it happily. He never showed affection in public.

He climbed into the car and went to sleep. He had the gift of instant relaxation. He didn't look his age by ten years, and Agnes, though she didn't wake him, held his hand between her own and waited.

She waited until they reached the villa, where her husband woke up and shook his shoulders. "Home," he said.

"I'm delighted you think so."

"Home is where you hang your hat. In point of fact, I left mine on that aircraft."

"Home is where a man has his breakfast."

"Point taken. I'd be glad of a good one."

She made him a generous English breakfast, and he ate it with an evident gusto. When he had finished he pushed his plate away. He wasn't a man who indulged in apologies, but he was always prepared to explain his actions.

"You caught me at rather short notice yesterday. I hope it doesn't sound like self-pity, but I stayed up most of the night to fix things. Then I didn't get a wink on that aircraft. An hour in the car . . ." He shrugged and smiled.

"So what you want is your bed?"

"I'll be useless without it."

"Do you mind if I join you?"

"I'd ardently hoped for it."

Agnes woke at three in the afternoon and stretched in a happy languor like a cat. She slipped down to make tea and brought it to William. "Six hours," she told him. "You've had a fair ration."

"Five hours if you deduct the irrelevant."

"I don't call that irrelevant."

"Good."

She saw he was refreshed and vigorous. "Now I'll tell you why I sent for you."

"Right."

She told him her story crisply and succinctly. At the end he said simply, "There's something missing."

"I'm afraid I'm not with you."

"That inspector gave you time—first a fortnight and then, you tell me, a week. He *gave* you that, but why I don't know. *Timeo Danaos et dona ferentes.*"

She'd heard that one and translated it back to him: "I fear Greeks bearing gifts."

"Correct. If his case had been cast iron, he'd have run you straight out. That spy story wouldn't stand up for long, not if I went to the High Commission. All diplomats have damp ears, that's an axiom, and the lot we have here in the island's capital are wetter than a baby's nappy. Just the same, they could hardly stand for that. Not, if I may say so with modesty, not for the wife of Sir William Withers. But this isn't just bluff, or not bluff all through. They mean to get you out all right."

"Then what's going to happen next?"

"I don't know that, but I'll stay till I do."

"But you can hardly hang around here indefinitely. Your work—"

"Can, as it happens, wait a while. In any case I think you forget something."

"What do I forget, then? Tell me."

He said on a note of affectionate irony, "You forget that your family made me marry you."

"What a four-letter man you are."

"But your husband."

The development William Withers had looked for came quickly and in an unusual form. It was the sound of angry women lamenting. The language was presumably Turkish, but it might have been French or Chinese or Hindi. The noise of a female altercation was unvarying across the world.

They put on dressing gowns and went down to the kitchen. The maid was there and two other women. The maid held a cleaver, doing most of the shouting, and the other two sat on chairs and wept. Occasionally they wailed in unison, a sort of classical chorus underscoring the maid. She was waving the cleaver and bawling, "I'll kill him."

William Withers said, "For God's sake quieten them."

Agnes knew better; she touched the maid's arm. "And whom are you going to kill, my dear?"

"That Inspector, that fiend from hell—"

"Quite so. But hadn't you better tell me first? If you're doing it in my time, that is."

The maid let a last despairing shriek, then sat down on a chair. Agnes took the chopper from her.

"They've cut off my father's water. Old Zekky."

Agnes translated; she knew it was serious. She was also very angry indeed. The usual swindle, she thought —it had happened before. They cooked up some preposterous claim, then they went to a court and took out an injunction. They did if they were also Greeks. Then a padlock went on the sluice in question and the owner of the land had had it. He'd be lucky if he could sell for tuppence.

William Withers had been thinking coolly; he said in the end. "So that's the real ploy—not spies but water. Old Zekky first, then that odious Englishwoman. It all falls into place very neatly. They're going to squeeze us out with the water." He considered again. "How much does the tank hold, the one on the roof?"

"Four days perhaps."

"Then we'd better be careful."

"What can we do?"

"You could let me think."

He settled to do so, but not for long. There was another violent interruption, men this time, but only slightly less strident. They began to shout too, and the maid collapsed finally. Agnes stood still and listened silently.

"They've got Zekky in prison."

"That's really outrageous." Sir William was getting angry too. "But they must have had some excuse."

"They had. You know he's a little bit 'round the bend, and when they stole his water he went the whole way. If he couldn't have water, nobody else should. So he goes to our conservatory and pinches all those tins we had there; he climbs up the hill to that grille in the rock face, where the water comes out—"

"I know it, I've walked there."

"Then he breaks the grille down and throws the tins in. Plenty of people saw him do it. They've arrested him for poisoning the water."

"Preposterous," Sir William said promptly. "That stuff was fungicides and garden sprays which some fool in his garden might perhaps use improperly, but in a solution of millions of gallons of water it wouldn't poison an ant, far less a man. Besides, he's very clearly dotty."

"So much the better for them. He'll be certified. Then what sort of a chance will he have in a lawsuit?"

"From what you've told me before, he hadn't one anyway."

"But we've got to get Zekky out. That inspector—"

"We have to consider our own water, too." He was mildly reproving, but only mildly. "Poisoning," he said softly. "Poisoning. Now that's an idea, and it might just work."

"What are you going to do?"

"Play my name. If it doesn't sound disagreeably pompous, I do have a certain reputation."

"I know that you could poison half Europe."

"Precisely the point." He rose in decision. "Now get this rabble out of here and bring me a jar of treacle or honey. I shall also want a fair-sized paint brush."

"But Willie, how—"

"Woman, be quiet."

It was a tone he seldom used to her, but when he did she jumped like a corporal.

"And get that inspector down here quickly. Tell him there's been a cosmic disaster."

The inspector arrived, but condescendingly. Agnes was Dutch and literally minded, and since her husband had used the words *cosmic disaster*, she'd repeated them when she rang the inspector. He hadn't been anywhere near believing them, but he'd understood the position perfectly. Or had thought he had, and it went like this: he'd been putting much pressure on Agnes Withers, so she'd sent for Sir William to plead her case. That was natural and he'd half expected it, but there was nothing her husband could say or do which would change his own intention, indeed his orders. On the other hand Sir William was eminent: it might look bad if he simply declined to see him.

William Withers for his part had set up the props. He wore his heaviest horn-rimmed spectacles and a formal suit which he kept at the villa for the very rare occasions he needed it. Since he was going to play the establishment scientist, it was proper to look like a Greek's idea of one, not the husband of an unpopular woman on what amounted to his forty-fourth honeymoon.

He greeted the inspector courteously, but wasted no time on spies or his wife.

"Come into the garden, please."

It was polite, but it had the ring of authority. The inspector was surprised but went with him. There was something about this solemn Englishman, the authentic aura of serious business. William Withers walked to a bush of hibiscus.

"I'd like you to look at that very carefully."

"A fine plant," the inspector said. He was puzzled. This wasn't working out his way. No apologies, no pleading, no bribes. He could have dealt with all three but not a lesson in gardening.

"I said carefully," Sir William said. Making his point, he turned a leaf. He had put on rubber gloves before doing so. On the back was a blob of viscous stain. The inspector touched it.

"Don't do that." The voice had been sharp with an urgent warning.

"What is it, then?"

"It's KD–27, I fear." William Withers was modestly proud of that; he'd invented it as he'd been changing his clothes.

"What's that?"

"It's a killer."

"You mean it could kill me?" He had noticed the gloves.

"Improbable, but it's still a killer, so it's very unwise to risk spreading it carelessly. It kills plants and trees and crops, not men." Withers waved at the smiling slopes below them. "In a month all that will be screaming desert."

The inspector was silent, thinking hard, for he knew where Sir William worked and at what. He hadn't believed him yet but was doubting. William Withers began to drive the doubt home. He did it smoothly and with increasing confidence, for he had taken the inspector's measure. This man had some formal education, and men with a formal education which was also not one in the world of science were more vulnerable to mumbo jumbo than the most ignorant peasant with no schooling at all.

"This disease does not occur in nature. It has to be induced by chemicals."

The inspector went up like a premature rocket. "That Zekky! I'll make him pay with his life."

Sir William Withers spread his gloved hands. "I

cannot pretend to understand it." He sounded sincere and solemn—behind these scared; he'd been an amateur actor of notable competence. "This blight is produced by a deadly defoliant. The Americans used it a lot in Vietnam."

"Christ," the inspector said. He crossed himself. He did it right to left. He was Orthodox.

"But you must not misunderstand me, inspector. To produce a defoliant useful in war you need laboratories, biochemicals, breeders—the sort of secret and sinister setup where I work myself at my own shameful trade."

"Then this has nothing to do with Zekky's foolishness?"

"I did not say that. I cannot say it."

The inspector was very severely shaken. "Then what are you trying to tell me, please?"

"I am telling you what any good scientist would. The first rule of science is nonomniscience. If you'd asked me if it was possible to produce an utterly deadly defoliant from a mixture of tins of commercial insecticides, I'd have said that no man had so far done so and offered you odds of ten thousand to one. But I've sufficient scientific discipline never to use the word *impossible.*"

The inspector sat down on a wooden bench. He looked at the land below him. He wept.

Sir William lit a cigarette. He smoked seldom and only out of doors. Agnes hated it and, as he'd said, he had discipline. When the inspector had finished crying, he gaffed him.

"No antidote, alas, is known." It was a statement, but held a note of uncertainty. The inspector caught it.

"None whatever?"

"I use words with precision. I said 'known,' not 'exists.' "

The inspector raised his hands in a sort of prayer. "In the name of God, of His Mother, the Saints . . ."

William Withers exhaled his smoke deliberately. "You put me in an appalling dilemma. Naturally if one finds such a thing, it's a secret of the utmost importance. I'd be in breach of a dozen regulations to say nothing of my professional conscience if I even considered unauthorised use of it. Nevertheless . . ."

He broke off; he was pacing it.

"Please," the inspector said. "I beg of you. I beg you in the name of my people."

"With whom my wife has lived in amity." He knew that she hadn't, but that wasn't the point. "She and her servants, one of them senile." He was too clever to state his terms and humiliate.

Nor did he need to. "I quite understand, sir."

"Then I'll telephone to England at once and enough will be on a flight tomorrow. You dissolve it in water and spray from an aircraft. Of course there may be procedural difficulties. I told you this was highly secret so it cannot travel alone, without escort. And it will probably be a commercial flight so the escort will have to be armed as well."

Young Watson would do it, he thought, and love it. It was exactly the sort of black joke he enjoyed.

"There'll be no trouble at the airport. None."

43

"Good." They shook hands. "I wish you well. And I hardly need stress the need for secrecy."

He went back into the house and to Agnes. "Zekky will be out quite soon. Don't pester him, just let him potter. And I don't think you'll hear any more about spying."

She opened her mouth but shut it quickly. He had used that voice an hour ago, and she knew what it meant. It meant No Questions.

He woke her in the night with laughter. For of course they wouldn't play fair, they were Greeks. They'd spray the stuff in a tearing hurry, some concoction of harmless household chemicals, but it was supposed to be a Great State Secret and there was money in any sort of secret. So sooner or later they'd have some analysed . . .

He laughed again, for it wouldn't matter. In his work he needed the best information, and from the latest he thought the Turks were coming. A week or maybe ten days at the most.

When Agnes would do something silly. She'd run up the Turkish flag and join them; she might even ask for arms to fight. When they'd promptly lock her up as a nuisance.

Sir William Withers rolled over contentedly. She'd get out all right—he could fix all that—but a week in a Turkish cell might sober her.

Or maybe it wouldn't. He reversed his position. Living the way they did they were happy.

Commentary on Timeo Danaos

WILLIAM HAGGARD

THIS STORY was written after a holiday in Cyprus which
produced more shock than pleasure. I knew that the
Turks were in a minority but did not know that they
were treated as helots in an island which had once
been part of their own proud empire. Every Greek I
met was uneasily proclaiming that Turkey would never
dare intervene. To me it seemed obvious that she
would; and she did.

It is a pleasure to recall that the State Department for once got it dead right. It issued a cool little statement deploring the use of American-donated weapons in a private war and thereafter did nothing that mattered. The British were even cooler. It is at least arguable that they were treaty-bound to go to war with Turkey, but they sat on their hands and stared out of the window. Both were exercises in classic realpolitik.

For despite a noisy Greek lobby in the United States, the simple fact is that Turkey is a valuable ally of NATO, Greece almost worthless. The commander of the American Sixth Fleet would hardly lose sleep if he heard that the entire Greek navy had sunk at anchor overnight; and any soldier would much prefer one stolid Turk, the formidable *mehmetchik,* to a platoon of quarreling Hellenes obsessed by a past which has gone forever.

The story wasn't written to convey a message, and if one can be read into it, it is nothing new. *Timeo Danaos et dona ferentes*—'I fear Greeks bearing gifts.' Or bearing anything else for that matter, particularly the military begging bowl. To fill it is a waste of precious arms. At the first sign of real trouble Greece will let both Britain and the United States down, as I privately fear that France will too.

After the Thin Man: Part I

DASHIELL HAMMETT

NBM *is honored to have the opportunity to publish for the first time Dashiell Hammett's original story on which the 1936 movie* After the Thin Man *was based.*

It is commonly believed that Hammett's writing career ended with the completion of his fifth novel, The Thin Man, *in 1933 and that he never again produced a long work of fiction. Not so. In fact, Hammett wrote two long original pieces after 1933:* After the Thin Man, *115 pages in typescript; and* Another Thin Man, *144 pages in typescript. Both of them were written as screen stories, the story line on which a screenplay is based.*

There were six movies in the Thin Man *series starring William Powell as Nick Charles and Myrna Loy as Nora. Beginning in 1934 with* The Thin Man, *based on Hammett's novel, the series spanned thirteen years and included* After the Thin Man *(1936),* Another Thin Man *(1939),* Shadow of the Thin Man *(1941),* The Thin Man Goes Home *(1944), and* Song of the Thin Man *(1947). The screenplays for the first three movies in the series were by Hammett's friends Albert Hackett and Frances Goodrich; the last three were produced without consultation with Hammett, and each of them employed different writers.*

Hammett's association with MGM was stormy. After the success of the movie The Thin Man *in 1934, a wire was sent from the Culver City office of MGM to the New York office requesting that*

47

Hammett be hired to write a sequel. Despite Louis B. Mayer's warning about Hammett's "irregular habits," a contract was negotiated by which Hammett was paid $2000 a week for ten weeks to write original story material. Hammett arrived in Culver City on October 29, 1934, rented a six-bedroom penthouse at the Beverly Wilshire Hotel, and proceeded to astonish Hollywood regulars with his profligacy. Two days after arriving in Hollywood, Hammett wrote Lillian Hellman that he had been doing "a little town roaming" until 5 A.M. and had begun work on his Thin Man sequel at ten that morning. The town roaming became habitual. He drank the nights away in the company of a variety of female partners and then complained about being harassed by starlets; he rarely went to the studio and frequently refused to talk by phone or even to correspond with director W. S. Van Dyke or producer Hunt Stromberg; and at the end of his ten-week contract, he had only a thirty-four-page plot summary to show.

The material was promising enough, however, to induce MGM to offer Hammett a new long-term contract which provided for a salary of $1000 a week to work as a script doctor and $1750 a week when he was working on "complete continuity." As Stromberg put it in a memo: "If Hammet ever sobers up and becomes fit to work, we would then have exclusive call on his services." The contract included a cancellation clause that allowed the studio to fire him with one week's notice, and they were forced to exercise that right at least once before After the Thin Man was completed, rehiring him within a week.

The screen story published here is Hammett's second draft. After his thirty-four-page summary was accepted, Hackett and Goodrich prepared a script. Hammett then revised the plot line, working from that script. There was a final revise before the movie was shot (*the changes will be discussed at the end of the second part of* After the Thin Man *in NBM6*), *but in most respects the movie follows the story published here.*

After the Thin Man *was released on Christmas Day 1936, with James Stewart playing David, Elissa Landi as Selma, and Joseph Calleia as Dancer. When the movie was released, the studio heads decided that while they wanted to continue the* Thin Man *series, they were no longer willing to be forced to accept Hammett's behavior because of his ownership of literary rights to the series' characters. So in February 1937, MGM agreed to pay Hammett $40,000 for all rights in perpetuity "to write and use, and cause to be written and used, stories . . . which contain any or all of the characters" in the motion pictures* The Thin Man *and* After the Thin Man. *Hammett worked sporadically for MGM during the next two years, but his only produced work was the third* Thin Man *movie. In a sullen mood after an argument with Hunt Stromberg during his work on that project, Hammett wrote to Lillian Hellman: "Maybe there are better writers in the world, but nobody ever invented a more insufferably smug pair of characters. They can't take that away from me even for $40,000."*

NOTE: *Transitional material (italicized in brackets) has been supplied by the editors.*

[THE ACTION *begins on board a train from New York as it pulls into San Francisco. It is New Year's Eve, and the Charleses are returning home just after Nick has solved* The Thin Man *case. They are met at the train by a gaggle of reporters congratulating Nick on his recent success as a detective and asking if he will continue his career as a private eye. His answer is a flat no.*

When they reach their palatial home, Nick and Nora find a boisterous New Year's Eve and welcome-home party in progress and join it unrecognized, as most of the guests do not know them.]

On SOUND TRACK, three pistol reports from front door, followed by the sound of door crashing back against wall and a man's hoarse exclamation.

Nick, followed by Nora, goes to the front door. The man who admitted them to the house—sober now—is standing at the door staring down with horrified face at a dead man huddled on the vestibule floor at his feet. The man at the door turns his frightened face to Nick and gasps, "I opened the door—bang, bang—he said 'Mees Selma Young' and fell down like that."

Nick corrects him mechanically—"Bang, bang, bang"—while kneeling to examine the man on the floor. He rises again almost immediately, saying, "Dead." By now guests and servants are crowding around them. Nora, craning her neck to look past Nick at the dead man's face, exclaims, "Nick, it's Pedro!"

Nick: "Who is Pedro?"

Nora: "You remember. Pedro Dominges—used to be Papa's gardener."

Nick says, "Oh, yes," doubtfully, looking at Pedro again. Pedro is a lanky Portuguese of fifty-five, with a pleasant, swarthy face and a gray handlebar mustache. Nick addresses the butler, "Phone the police, Peters." Then he turns to discover that the man who opened the door has tiptoed past the corpse and is now going

50

down the steps to the street. "Wait a minute," Nick calls. The man turns around on the bottom step and says very earnestly, "Listen, I . . . , I . . . This kind of thing upsets me. I got to go home and lay down."

Nick looks at the man without saying anything, and the man reluctantly comes back up the steps complaining, "All right, brother, but you're going to have a sick man on your hands."

A little man, obviously a crook of some sort, plucks at Nick's elbow and whines, "You got to let *me* out, Nick. You know I'm in no spot to be messing with coppers right now."

Nick: "You should have thought of that before you shot him."

The little man jumps as if he had been kicked.

During this scene a crowd has been gradually assembling in the street around the door: first a grocer's delivery boy, then a taxi driver, pedestrians, etc. Now a policeman pushes his way through the crowd, saying, "What's going on here?" and comes up the steps. He salutes Nick respectfully and says, "How do you do, Mr. Charles? Glad to see you back," then sees the dead man and goggles at him.

Nick: "We called in."

The policeman goes down the steps and begins to push the crowd around, growling, "Get back there! Get back there!" In the distance a police siren can be heard.

Indoors, a few minutes later, Lieutenant Abrams of the police homicide detail—who looks somewhat like an older version of Arthur Caesar—is saying to Nora,

"You're sure of the identification, Mrs. Charles? He's the Pedro Dominges that used to be your gardener?"

Nora: "Absolutely sure."

Abrams: "How long ago was that?"

Nora: "Six years at least. He left a little before my father died."

Abrams: "Why'd he leave?"

Nora: "I don't know."

Abrams: "Ever see him since?"

Nora: "No."

Abrams: "What did he want here?"

Nora: "I don't know. I—"

Abrams: "All right. Thanks." He speaks to one of his men: "See what you can get." The man goes to a phone in another room. (In this scene, the impression to be conveyed is that Abrams has already asked his preliminary questions and is now patiently going over the same ground again, checking up, filling in details.)

Abrams turns to the guests: "And none of you admit you know him, huh?" Several of them shake their heads, the others remain quiet.

Abrams: "And none of you know a Miss Selma Young?"

There is the same response.

Abrams: "All right." Then, more sharply: "Mullen, have you remembered anything else?"

The man who had opened the door runs his tongue over his lips and says, "No, sir. It's just like I told you. I went to the door when it rang, thinking it was maybe some more guests, or maybe them"—nodding at Nick and Nora—"and then there was the shots and he kind of gasped what sounded to me like 'Mees Selma Young' and he fell down dead like that. I guess there was an automobile passing maybe—I don't know."

Abrams, aside to Nick: "Who is he?"

Nick: "Search me."

Abrams to Mullen: "Who are you? What were you doing here?"

Mullen, hesitantly: "I come to see about buying a puppy and somebody give me a drink and—" His face lights up and he says with enthusiasm, "It was a *swell* party. I never—"

Abrams interrupts him: "What are you doing answering the doorbell if you just chiseled in?"

Mullen, sheepishly: "Well, I guess I had a few drinks and was kind of entering in the spirit of the thing."

Abrams addresses one of his men: "Take good-time Charlie out to where he says he lives and works and find out about him." The man takes Mullen and goes out.

In another room, the detective at the phone is saying, "Right, Mack. I got it." He hangs up. As he reaches the door, the phone rings. He glances around, goes softly back to it.

In the hallway, the butler answers the phone: "Mr. Charles's residence. . . . Yes, Mrs. Landis. . . . Yes, ma'am." He goes into the room where the others are and speaks aside to Nora: "Mrs. Landis is on the telephone, ma'am."

Nora goes to the phone, says, "Hello, Selma. How are you, dear?"

Selma, in hat and street clothes, her face wild, cries hysterically: "Nora, you and Nick have simply got to come tonight! Something terrible has happened! I don't know what to . . . I'll kill myself if . . . You've got to! If you don't, I'll—" She breaks off as she sees Aunt Katherine standing in the doorway looking sternly at her. Aunt Katherine is very old but still big-boned and powerful, with a grim, iron-jawed face. She, too, is in hat and street clothes, and she leans on a thick cane. Selma catches her breath in a sob and says weakly, "Please come."

Nora, alarmed: "Certainly we'll come, dear. We'll do—"

Selma says hastily, "Thanks," and hangs up, avoiding Aunt Katherine's eyes. Aunt Katherine, not taking her eyes from Selma, puts out a hand and rings a bell, saying when a servant comes in, "A glass of water." Both women remain as they are in silence until the servant returns with the water. Then Aunt Katherine takes the water from the servant, takes a tablet from a small bottle in her own handbag, and with water in one hand, tablet in the other, goes to Selma and says, "Take this and lie down until time for dinner."

Selma objects timidly: "No, Aunt Katherine, please. I'm all right. I'll be quite all right."

Aunt Katherine: "Do as I say—or I shall call Dr. Kammer."

Selma slowly takes the tablet and water.

The detective at Nick's who has been listening on the extension quickly puts down the phone and, returning to the room where the others are, calls Abrams aside and whispers into his ear, telling him what he overheard. While this is going on, Nora returns and tells Nick, "You're in for it, my boy. I promised Selma we'd come to Aunt Katherine's for dinner tonight. I had to. She's so upset she—"

Nick: "That means outside of putting up with the rest of your family, we'll have to listen to her troubles with Robert. I won't—"

Nora, coaxingly: "But you like Selma."

Nick: "Not that much."

Nora: "Please, Nicky."

Nick: "I won't go sober."

Nora pats his cheek: "You're a darling."

Abrams comes back from his whispered conference with the other detective and says, "Mrs. Charles, I'll have to ask you who you were talking to on the phone."

Nora, puzzled: "My cousin, Selma Landis."

Abrams: "She married?"

Nora: "Yes."

Abrams: "What was her last name before she was married?"

Nora: "Forrest, the same as mine."

Abrams: "She ever go by the name of Young?"

Nora: "Why no! Surely you don't think—" She looks at Nick.

Abrams: "What was she so excited about?"

Nora, indignantly: "You listened?"

Abrams, patiently: "We're policemen, Mrs. Charles, and a man's been killed here. We got to try to find out what goes on the best way we can. Now, is there any connection between what she was saying and what happened here?"

Nora: "Of course not. It's probably her husband."

Abrams: "You mean this fellow that was killed?"

Nick: "There's a thought!" He asks Nora solemnly, "Do you suppose Selma was ever married to Pedro?"

Nora: "Stop it, Nick." Then to Abrams: "No, no. It's her husband she was talking about."

Abrams nods: "Maybe that's right. I can see that. I'm a married man myself." After a moment's thought he asks, "Did she know this fellow that was killed?"

Nora: "I suppose so. She and my husband and her husband were all friends and used to come there before any of us were married."

Abrams: "Then her husband might know him too, huh?"

Nora: "He might."

Abrams turns to Nick: "How come you didn't recognize him before Mrs. Charles told you?"

Nick: "Who notices a gardener unless he squirts a hose on you?"

Abrams: "There's something in that. I remember once when—Well, never mind." He addresses the detective who phoned: "Find out anything about Dominges?"

The detective: "Did a little bootlegging before repeal—bought hisself an apartment house at 346 White Street—lives there and runs it hisself. Not married. No record on him."

Abrams asks the assembled company: "346 White

Street mean anything to anybody?" Nobody says it does. He asks his men: "Got all their names and addresses?"

"Yes."

Abrams: "All right. You people can clear out. We'll let you know when we want to see you again."

The guests start to leave as if glad to go, especially a little group of men who have been herded into a corner by a couple of policemen, but this group is halted by one of the policemen, who says, "Take it easy, boys. We've got a special wagon outside for you. We been hunting for some of you for months." They are led out between policemen.

Abrams, alone in the room with Nick and Nora, looks at Nick: "Well?"

Nick says, "Oh, sure," and begins to mix drinks.

Abrams: "I didn't mean that exactly. I mean what do you make all this add up to? He's killed coming to see you. He knows you two and Mrs. Charles's relations, and that's all we know he does know. What do you make of it?"

Nick, handing him a drink: "Maybe he was a fellow who didn't get around much."

[*Nick and Nora go to Aunt Katherine's for dinner. The party is composed of stodgy, aged family members with the exception of Selma, who is morose. After dinner, Nick and the men stay at table; the women retire to the parlor, where Selma entertains them by playing the piano. Nora, seated next to Selma, asks her in a whisper what is wrong. When she starts to answer, Aunt Katherine demands that she continue to play.*]

Selma puts her hands to her face and runs from the room to the library beyond, while Aunt Katherine rises to her feet and the other women look wide-eyed and alarmed. Nora says, "Let me talk to her," and goes out after Selma.

In the library, Selma is sobbing on a sofa. Nora sits down beside her, puts her arms around her, says, "Don't, dear. Nick'll find Robert for you. I'm sure he's just—"

Selma sits up, pushing Nora's arms away, crying hysterically: "Sometimes I hate you and Nick. You're so happy together, and here Robert and I haven't been married half as long and I'm so miserable. I wish he'd never come back. I wish he were dead. I don't really love him. I never did, really. I was a fool to have married him instead of David." She puts her head on Nora's shoulder and begins to sob again.

Nora, stroking Selma's hair: "Well then, dear, divorce him. Don't let Aunt Katherine keep you from that. If you—"

Selma raises her head again: "But I'm such a fool. This is the first time he's gone off like this without a word, without even telling me lies about where he's going, but there have always been other women and I've always known it. But I've let him twist me around his little finger and made myself believe his lies even when I knew they were lies and—he doesn't love me. He married me for my money. Yet he does horrible things to me, and then when I see him I let him smooth everything over and I want to think we love each other and everything will turn out all right. And it won't, it won't. It's all lies and I'm a fool. Oh, why didn't I marry David?" She bursts into tears again.

Meanwhile Aunt Katherine has come into the library and shut the door. Now she says coldly, "You *are* a fool, Selma, but you might have the decency not to scream so the servants will find out exactly what *kind* of fool you are."

"Aunt Katherine!" Nora protests. "Selma's not well. She—"

Aunt Katherine interrupts her, nodding her head grimly: "I know she's not well. I know better than anyone else—except Doctor Kammer—how far from being well she really is." Selma flinches. Aunt Katherine says to Nora, "Will you ask Nicholas to come in?" Nora hesitates as if about to say something, then goes out. Aunt Katherine says to Selma, "Fix yourself up. You look like Ophelia." Selma flinches again and begins to fix her hair, dress, etc.

[*When Nora goes to the dining room to summon Nick, she finds him in mock conversation with the rest of the men, who are all snoring comically. As Nick leaves the table, he places a floral centerpiece in the hands of one of them.*]

Nick and Nora are going through the hallway. She is holding his arm and seems worried. She says, "Aunt Katherine wants to see you."

Nick: "What have I done now?"

Nora: "Do you know why Robert wasn't here tonight?"

Nick: "Because he's smart."

Nora: "I'm not fooling. He's disappeared."

Nick: "That's swell. Now if we can get rid of—"

Nora: "Be nice to Selma, Nicky. She's having such a tough time of it."

Nick stops and turns Nora around to face him, looking at her with suspicion. He says, "Now come on, tell the old man. What are you getting him into?"

Nora, paying no attention to this: "And do try to be polite to Aunt Katherine. It'll make it easier for Selma."

Nick sighs deeply, and they go into the library.

[*Nick questions Selma under Aunt Katherine's watchful gaze about her problem, and she tells him the circumstances of Robert's disappearance.*]

Selma: "Our names might get in the papers. People might find out that I'm married to a drunken wastrel, a thief, a man who's already cost me a small fortune getting him out of scrapes with women, a man who has never done a decent thing in—"

Aunt Katherine raps with her cane on the floor and says, "Selma, stop that nonsense!"

Selma puts her hands over her face and cries, "I don't care what anybody knows, I don't care what gets in the papers, if I can only be happy once again."

Nora goes to her to soothe her.

Aunt Katherine, quietly: "We've kept our private affairs out of the public print up until now, and I hope we shall continue to do so." She smiles at Nick as if conferring a favor on him. "I shall leave it in your hands, Nicholas. I know you'll welcome a chance to help us, and I needn't tell you how grateful we'll be if you see that Robert returns home without any scandal." She smiles at Nora, says, "If you'll forgive me, I'll go back to my guests. When you've quieted Selma, I think she'd better go off to bed." She goes out calmly and majestically.

Nick, looking after her half-admiringly, half-disgustedly: "Katherine the Great!"

Selma comes over to Nick, holding out her hands: "I don't know how to thank you, Nick."

Nick takes her hands: "You mean you don't know what to thank me for. What is all this fiddledeedee?"

Selma: "Robert hasn't been home. I haven't seen or heard from him for three days."

Nick: "Where do you think he might be?"

Selma: "I don't know. It's some woman, of course. It gets worse and worse. Only last week some Chinese restaurant—Lichee or something—sent me a cigarette case they thought I'd left there, and I know it was some woman that was there with him, though he swore it wasn't."

Nick: "Well, you're at least a cigarette case ahead—or wasn't it worth keeping?"

Nora says, "Nick," reprovingly, while Selma, not knowing he is kidding her, says, "I sent it back, of course, with a note saying it wasn't mine, but I don't—" She breaks off to look at the butler, who is standing in the doorway.

The butler says, "A—ah—gentleman from the police to see you, Mrs. Landis."

Selma screams and faints.

Selma's scream brings in Aunt Katherine, followed by the rest of the family. During the ensuing hubbub, while they are bringing her to, asking each other what happened, Lieutenant Abrams comes in. He nods at Nick, says, "I thought maybe you'd be here," looks at Selma, and asks, "Is the lady in trouble Mrs. Selma Landis?"

Nick: "Yes."

Abrams: "I thought maybe it was." Then, to Nora, who is now looking at him: "Evening, Mrs. Charles."

By this time the others have noticed him. Aunt Katherine looks inquiringly at him. Nick introduces them elaborately: "Miss Forrest, may I present Lieutenant Abrams of the Police Department homicide detail?"

Aunt Katherine asks sharply, "Homicide?"

Selma pushes past her to put her hands on Abrams's arms, demanding, "What has happened to him?"

Abrams (as always, in a manner that may come from stupidity, or may come from a shrewd pretense of stupidity): "He was killed this afternoon. Didn't Mr. Charles tell you?"

Selma stares at him in dumb horror.

Nora: "He doesn't mean Robert, dear. He means Pedro, the gardener we used to have. You remember him." She helps Selma to a chair, then asks Abrams indignantly, "Did you do that on purpose?"

Aunt Hattie: "I can't understand a thing that's going on." She points at Abrams: "Is this man a burglar? Why doesn't someone call the police?"

Abrams addresses Nick: "You didn't tell 'em about Pedro being killed?"

Nick: "This is my wife's family. They'd think I did it."

Abrams: "I see what you mean. My wife's got relations, too."

The butler appears in the doorway and says, "Mr. David Graham to see Mrs. Landis." Selma starts up from her chair.

Aunt Katherine says, "I think it better that we be home to no one but members of the family this evening."

Selma protests, "I want to see David. Ask him to come in, Henry."

The butler remains in the doorway, looking at Aunt Katherine, who says, "Selma, I don't want to have to—"

Before she has finished this threat, David comes in hurriedly, going straight to Selma and asking, "What is it? What's the matter?"

Aunt Katherine replies coldly, "That is exactly what we'd like to know. Something is said about a gardener being killed and Selma becomes hysterical."

David: "A gardener? What's that got to do with Selma?"

Lieutenant Abrams: "Excuse me, but that's what we're trying to find out. This man is killed coming to see Mr. and Mrs. Charles, and a little while later Mrs. Landis phones all excited and talking about killing herself and—"

David, angrily: "And on the strength of that you come here to annoy her?"

Abrams, patiently: "Not only that. Mrs. Charles said she," indicating Selma, "knew him, and how are we going to get anywhere if we don't talk to the people that knew him?"

Nora: "I didn't say she knew him. I said she might remember him." She turns to David: "It was Pedro who used to work for Papa when we had the place in Ross."

David: "Oh, yes. I remember him, a tall man with a long, gray mustache. But what—"

Abrams: "So you knew him, too. Well, what do you know about him?"

David: "Nothing. I merely saw him when I was a visitor there, and I've never seen him since."

Abrams: "And you, Mrs. Landis?"

Selma: "I may have seen him, but I don't remember him at all."

Abrams: "And how about the rest of you?"

None of the Forrests admits knowing Pedro.

Abrams: "Mrs. Charles says Mrs. Landis's husband might know him. Is he here?"

Selma: "No. He . . . he'll be in later, but I don't think he'll remember the man any better than I do."

Abrams: "Did you ever go by the name of Selma Young?"

Selma: "Certainly not!"

Abrams: "Anybody here know Selma Young?"

Nobody does.

Abrams: "Now I got to ask you again about that telephone talk of yours with Mrs. Charles."

Selma: "Please, it had nothing to do with this. It was . . . was a purely personal thing."

Abrams: "You mean something to do with your husband?"

Aunt Katherine: "Mr. . . . ah . . . Abraham, you are being impertinent. Furthermore, my niece is under a doctor's care, and—"

Abrams, stolidly: "What doctor?"

Aunt Katherine: "Doctor Frederic Kammer."

Abrams nods: "I know of him." Preparing to leave, he says resignedly, "I can't help it if people don't like me. I got my work to do. Good night." He goes out.

(Note: David should leave house with Nick and Nora, parting from them in street. Foggy.)

When Nick and Nora leave, Nick asks Harold, the chauffeur, "Where's a good place to get the stink of respectability out of our noses?"

Harold, grinning and chewing his gum: "I get it. Well, there's Tim McCrumb's, and there's the Lichee, and there's the Tin Dipper. None of them three ain't apt to be cluttered up with schoolteachers."

Nick: "Suppose we try the Lichee."

Harold: "That's a good pick," while Nora looks at Nick from the corners of her eyes. As they get into the car she says, "You are going to find Robert?"

Nick: "*I* didn't lose him."

Nora: "It would put you in right with the family."

Nick: "And *that's* what I'm afraid of."

In Dancer's apartment at the Lichee Club, Robert, drunk and looking as if he has been drunk for several days, is lying back in a chair, holding a drink. Polly is sitting on the arm of his chair, running her fingers through his hair. He is saying, "Comes tomorrow and we'll be out of this town for good. No more wife squawking at me, no more of her family egging her on, no more of this," waving his glass around the place. "Just you and me off someplace together." He pulls her down in his lap and asks, "Good, baby?"

She says, "Swell." Then, "You're sure this—what's his name?—Graham—will come through all right?"

Robert: "Sure. He's nuts about Selma. He fell all over himself when I put it to him. The only thing is, maybe I was a sucker not to ask him for twice as much for clearing out. Don't worry about the money; he'll have it ready in the morning just as he promised."

Polly, reassured, asks thoughtfully, "Does she know about it?"

Robert, scornfully: "Of course not. He couldn't tell her. She's batty as a pet cuckoo. She'd blow up and make him call off the whole thing."

Polly: "Then suppose she finds out about it afterwards and won't marry him."

66

Robert: "Listen. This guy's a sap, and he's in love with her. He wants to marry her all right, but even if he knew there was no chance of that, he'd still pay me to clear out. He thinks I'm bad for her and he lo-o-ves her and wants her to be ha-a-ppy."

Polly laughs and kisses him, says, "If you want to hear me sing, you'd better come on out and find a table. I go on in a few minutes."

Outside the door, Phil has been listening. He turns away from the door not quite quickly enough as Dancer comes up behind him. Dancer says casually, "Catch a good earful?"

Phil: "I wanted to see Polly, but I didn't want to butt in if she was busy."

Dancer links an arm through Phil's and starts leading him away from the door toward the stairs, saying, "She's busy. She'll be busy all evening."

Phil hangs back, saying: "I got to see her for a minute."

Dancer jerks him along, says, still casually, "Not this evening. You shake her down for too much dough, Phil, even if she is your sister. Lay off her a while."

Phil pulls his arm free, says, "That's no skin off your face. If she wants to help me out a little, that's her business. Why shouldn't she? I know things that are going on around here that—"

Dancer reaches out, grabs him by the necktie, and pulls him close, saying softly, "Smart boy. You know things. When are you going to start shaking *me* down?"

Phil: "When I want to shake you down, I'll—"

Dancer stops him this time by slapping his face once, not especially hard. Dancer: "I don't like you, but I've put up with having you around because you're Polly's brother, and she's a nice kid, but don't think you can ride too far on that ticket." He puts his open hand over Phil's face, and pushes him backwards down the stairs, saying, "Now stay away for a couple of days."

Phil tumbles backwards into the arms of Nick, who, with Nora, is coming up the stairs. Nick says, "Mmmm! Big confetti they throw here."

Dancer exclaims, "Ah, Mr. Charles! I'm sorry!" and starts down the stairs.

Phil snarls at Nick: "Why don't you look where you're going, you big clown?" He twists himself out of Nick's arms and goes downstairs out of the place.

Dancer is apologizing again.

Nick: "Hello, Dancer. This your place? A neat way you have of getting rid of the customers."

Dancer smiles professionally: "Just a kid that hangs around because his sister works here. I get tired of him sponging on Polly sometimes."

Nick: "I felt a gun under his arm when I caught him."

Dancer, contemptuously: "Just breaking it in for a friend, I guess." He ushers them upstairs.

Outside the Lichee, Phil finds a dark doorway from which the club can be watched and plants himself there. Nick's car is parked near the doorway. Both Harold and a taxi driver who is talking to him see Phil, but neither pays much attention to the boy. Harold is chewing gum and listening with a bored air to the taxi driver, who is telling him,

"And I said to him, 'You ain't going to give me a ticket, you big flatfoot, and you know it,' I said. I said, 'I got a right to turn there, and you know it,' I said, 'and I ain't got all night to be sitting here gassing, so go polish your buttons and leave me be on my way, you fat palooka,' I said."

Harold, wearily: "I know, and then you busted out crying."

Upstairs in the Lichee, Nick is checking his hat and coat while Nora looks interestedly around the place. Suddenly she grabs Nick's arm, says, "There's Robert!"

Robert and Polly are going into the restaurant.

Nick: "The night's bulging with your family."

Nora starts to pull him toward Robert: "Come on."

Dancer to Nick: "Is Mr. Landis a friend of yours?"

Nick, as Nora drags him off: "On the contrary, a relation."

Dancer stares thoughtfully after them.

By the time Nick and Nora reach Robert, he and Polly are sitting at a small table near the orchestra. Nora holds out a hand to Robert, saying, "Hello, Robert," with a great show of cordiality. He rises drunkenly, mumbling, "Hello, Nora; hello, Nick," and shakes their hands. Then he introduces Polly: "Miss Byrnes, Mr. and Mrs. Charles." Nick immediately sits down and begins to talk to Polly, giving Nora a chance to speak aside to Robert.

Nick: "Anything for a laugh."

69

Nora, in a low voice to Robert: "You oughtn't to stay away like this."

Robert: "I know, but Selma's not easy to get along with, and sometimes I simply have to break loose."

Nora: "But you should let her know that you're all right."

Robert: "You're right, of course. But sit down. You can talk in front of Polly. She knows about Selma."

Polly, aside to Nick: "Tell Mrs. Charles not to worry about him. I'll see that he gets home tonight." She moves her foot under the table and touches Robert's. He starts to laugh, then covers his mouth with his hand. He asks, "Is—is Selma all right?"

Nora, indignantly: "You know she's not, and now with the police bothering her—"

Robert: "The police?" He and Polly both look alarmed.

Nora: "Yes, the idiots. A gardener we used to have was killed. Remember Pedro Dominges?"

Before Robert can reply, Polly exclaims: "Killed? Why, he's—" She breaks off with a hand to her mouth.

Nick prompts her: "He's what?"

Polly, to Nora: "What was his name?"

Nora: "Pedro Dominges."

Polly: "Oh! I thought you said Peter Dominger—a fellow I used to know."

Nick looks at her skeptically.

Robert: "What's that got to do with Selma?"

Nick: "Ask the police. They don't know. I wonder if our table's ready." He stands up.

Polly whispers, "I'll see he gets home all right."

Nick: "Thanks. Pleased to have metten up with you." He and Nora move off to where Dancer is beckoning them.

Polly leans over to Robert, speaking swiftly: "Honey, could you get hold of that guy Graham and see if you can get the money right away?"

Robert: "Maybe. Why?"

Polly: "I was thinking there's no sense in waiting until tomorrow. I'll tell Dancer I don't feel well and get the night off and we'll blow town right away. Would you like that?"

A waiter comes up with fresh drinks as Robert says, "I'll try him on the phone now."

[*Dancer shows Nick and Nora to their own table on the other side of the room, and there are comic encounters with New Year's Eve revelers. Polly sings on stage.*]

After her performance, Dancer goes to the table where Polly is now sitting alone and asks, "What's the setup?"

Polly: "They're Bobbie's cousins by marriage and think he ought to go home to his wife."

Dancer purses his lips thoughtfully for a moment then says, "It's all to the good, them seeing him here plastered, but I guess we can't take a chance on them tipping off the wife and having her bang in. Give the customers one song and knock off for the night. Take him up to your place."

Polly: "I'm getting kind of tired of him."

Dancer: "It's only till tomorrow night. You can turn him loose then. Put a pill in his drink when you get him home so he'll be sure to stay safe asleep while you run out to do that little errand in the morning." He pats her shoulder.

Polly, without enthusiasm: "All right." She gets up to sing.

Robert, at the telephone talking to David: "That money you promised me tomorrow. Give it to me tonight and I'll be half across the country by daylight."

David: "I told you I couldn't raise it till tomorrow."

Robert, snarling: "How'd you like it if I changed my mind between now and tomorrow?"

David: "But, Robert, I—" He breaks off as he thinks of something, then says, "I've got the bonds I was going to raise the money on—if you'll take them."

Robert: "They're negotiable? There's no foolishness about them?"

David: "Certainly they're negotiable! Do you think I'd—?"

Robert: "I don't think anything about you. How soon can you turn them over?"

David: "As soon as you can get here."

Robert: "I won't come there for them."

David: "All right. Where are *you*?"

Robert: "At the Lichee."

David: "Then I can meet you at the corner of .... and .... in ten minutes."

Robert: "OK, but don't keep me waiting, or I might change my mind."

David: "And you'll give me your word you'll—"

Robert: "I've got to go home and pack a bag, but I won't bother your sainted Selma. I won't even see her if I can get out of it." He slams the receiver on the hook, says "Boy Scout!" at it, and returns to his table. (Throughout this scene, waiters, etc. have been passing and repassing Robert at the phone, but none seems to have paid any attention to his conversation.)

Nick and Nora are at their table listening to Polly singing. Dancer, intent now on keeping them comfortable until Polly and Robert are safely away, comes to the table and asks, "Everything all right, Mr. Charles?"

Nick, shuddering at his first taste of his drink and frowning at the glass: "It's all something."

Dancer laughs with professional heartiness and addresses the waiter: "Ling, no check for this table. Anything they want is on the house."

Nick: "I can't let you do that."

Dancer: "But I insist. You must be my guest."

Nick, at this point seeing the approach of a group of thugs and realizing that somebody's going to be stuck for a lot of drinks, says quickly, "We accept with thanks. That's mighty good of you, Dancer." He shakes Dancer's hand as the thugs arrive and says, "Meet the rest of my party."

Eddie: "We don't want to meet him. He's a crumb."

Nick: "But he's giving the party. It's all on the house."

Eddie: "Well, I'll—well, well!" He turns to his companions, saying enthusiastically, "Boys! Champagne!"

Nick: "Certainly champagne."

Dancer tries to smile as if he likes it. The others crowd him back out of the way as they make room for themselves around the table.

[*There are comic scenes at Nick's table when he introduces Nora to his unsavory friends, who are celebrating Willie's release from prison. Everybody orders champagne except Eddie, who wants Scotch with a champagne chaser. When Willie orders his drinks, Nora says she'll have the same.*]

Polly, nearing the end of her song, looks questioningly at Robert, who nods and points to his watch and the door to indicate that she should hurry. Lum Kee is watching them. He goes over to Dancer, who has left Nick's table.

Lum Kee: "No trouble, Dancer. I ask you, please."

Dancer, putting a hand on his partner's arm: "Stop worrying, Lum. Everything's OK."

Lum Kee: "All the time you say everything OK. All the time trouble-trouble."

Dancer: "We always get out of it, don't we?"

Lum Kee: "You bet you, but too much money. Pretty soon money not fix something. Then no more Lichee."

Dancer slaps Lum Kee on the back and says, "If it's Landis you're worrying about, I'll tell him to stay away. I don't like the guy much either. But you'll find something else to squawk about."

Lum Kee, cheerfully: "You bet you."

Polly, having finished her song, tells the orchestra to play a dance number instead of an encore and goes toward her dressing room. She gives Nora a reassuring nod as she passes. Robert is getting his hat and coat. Dancer crosses to meet Polly at the door and says, "Just keep him in your apartment till evening, and we'll both be cutting ourselves a nice piece of gravy."

Polly, without enthusiasm: "I hope so. Has Phil been in tonight?"

Dancer: "For a minute. He went off like he had a date. Go ahead, kid." He pats her back, urging her toward the door. She goes out.

At Nick's table, his guests are still applauding Polly deafeningly, pounding the table with bottles, etc. Nora seems to be talking to Nick, but nothing can be heard. He yells back, "Can't hear you." The words are barely audible. She puts her mouth to his ear and screams, "Do you think that girl will really see that he gets home?"

The noise dies suddenly just as she starts, and everybody in the place looks at her; her scream could be heard a block away. Willie, who has been banging on the table with two bottles, nudges the thug beside him and says, "I don't care whose wife she is, I don't like a dame that gets noisy when she's had a few snifters."

Nick is trying to recover his hearing in the ear Nora

75

screamed in. She asks again, but in a lower voice, "Do you?"

Nick: "She'll see that he gets to somebody's home. You can phone if you want, when he's had time to get there."

Outside, the fog is thicker. Polly starts for a taxi, but Robert says, "It's only three blocks." They turn down the street. Phil comes out of his doorway and follows them. Harold is slumped down in the seat of Nick's car, asleep, though his jaws still move a little with his gum. The taxi driver is saying, "And I said to this truck driver, 'All right, tough guy, if you don't like me cutting in on you, how would you like to climb down off that hearse and get bopped in the nose?' I said."

At a corner three blocks from the Lichee, Robert points to David, waiting in his car, and says, "There's our honeymoon money!" Polly holds back as he goes toward the car, but he takes her arm, saying, "Come on. I want him to see how much better I'm doing." They go up to the car.

Robert: "Have you got the bonds?"

David slowly looks from one to the other of them as he takes a thick sheaf of bonds from his pocket. He hands them to Robert, who eagerly examines them then says, "Thanks, Sir Galahad," as he puts them into his pocket.

David: "You'll keep your promise?"

Robert: "Don't worry about that. And I wish you as much luck with your bargain as I got with mine." He pulls Polly toward him and kisses her on the mouth. David turns his head away in disgust. Robert laughs at him, says, "There's only one thing. I'm going home to pack a bag. Stay away till I've cleared out. Fifteen minutes oughtn't to mean anything to a man who's waited as long as you have. Ta-ta!" He and Polly turn away. David looks after them for a moment, then sighs as if with relief and slowly starts his car.

At Nick's table in the Lichee, Eddie is complaining: "Where's Polly? I want to hear Polly sing. We come up here and spend all this dough" (indicating the champagne bottles) "and what does she do? She sings one song and quits."

Joe, earnestly: "You can't say anything against Polly. She's all to the good."

Another thug, very drunk, his eyes almost shut: "She still live in that place on White Street with the ghosts running up and down the halls?"

Nora, very interested: "A haunted house?"

The drunk, opening his eyes: "Did I say ghosts? I'm drunk, lady. I meant goats." He puts fingers up to his head to imitate horns and says, "Ba-a-a!"

Nora: "Well, that's *almost* as good."

Nick, as if not very interested: "What part of White Street?"

The drunk: "346. I can always remember that number because my old man used to have a livery stable there."

At the mention of the number Nora puts her hand quickly on Nick's and looks at him with a frightened face. Nick pats her hand without taking his attention from the drunk and asks: "In the place with the goats?"

The drunk, who is going back to sleep, shakes his head and says, "No, that was back in Baraboo, Wisconsin."

Nick: "You know the fellow who owns the house?"

The drunk: "In Baraboo?"

Nick: "The one Polly lives in."

The drunk shakes his head again: "Nope, but he ought to keep the front door shut so the goats can't get in."

Nick: "He was killed today."

The drunk: "It don't surprise me. Stands to reason no tenants weren't going to put up with those goats forever." The other thugs exchange glances, then begin to regard Nick with suspicion.

Nora: "Nick, I'm going to phone."

Nick: "He's had time enough to get home." He holds out a handful of change.

Dancer, not far away, sees Nora take the nickel (if necessary, he can have overheard some of the conversation), and he goes quickly to one of the hatcheck girls and says, "Get on the phone and stay there." She goes to the phone, drops in a coin, and when Nora arrives the girl is in the middle of a long description of a dress (that can be written much more accurately by Miss Goodrich than by Mr. Hammett). Nora waits impatiently.

At Nick's table, his guests are no longer having a

good time; his questioning the drunk looks too much as if he were working on a murder job. Eddie clears his throat, says, "Well, boys, I guess we better be trucking along."

Willie: "I guess we better." Only the drunk seems comfortable.

Nick: "What's the matter? It's early. Don't you like the party?"

Eddie: "Sure we like it. It's swell. But, well, we got to get up early in the morning."

Nick: "Surely you haven't become an early riser in your old age, Eddie."

Eddie squirms: "Well, no, but—" He gets a bright idea: "You see, we're giving Willie a picnic. He's nuts about picnics and he's been locked up a long time, so we thought we'd take him out in the country early tomorrow morning and throw a picnic for him. Ain't that right, Willie?"

Willie: "I'm sure nuts about picnics!"

The drunk has opened his eyes and is staring at the others in surprise. He says, "What's the matter with you dopes? What can you lift out in the country?" Then more indignantly, "I ain't gonna ride in the back seat with no *cow!*"

Eddie laughs, says to Nick, "Ain't he a card!" and with Willie's help begins to haul the drunk to his feet.

Dancer, going into his apartment, says to a passing waiter, "Bring me a glass of milk." In his apartment, he goes to the telephone and calls Polly's number. Lum Kee is lying on a sofa reading a book. Dancer waits patiently at the phone until the waiter comes in with his milk, then he puts down the phone and says, "That bum! I told her to take him straight to her place."

Lum Kee, not looking up from his book: "Mr. Landis?"

Dancer: "Uh-huh. I wanted her to get him in shape so he could go home."

Waiter: "Mr. Landis on phone I hearum say go home pack bag."

Dancer's eyes narrow, then he says, "Oh, sure, that's right. I had forgotten."

The waiter goes out. Dancer stands idly spinning an ashtray on a table for a moment, then yawns and says, "I think I'll go out for a couple of minutes and get a little air in one of my lungs." Lum Kee nods without looking up. Dancer takes his hat and coat from a closet, says, "That last batch of Scotch we got from Monty's pretty bad."

Lum Kee: "I tell him."

Dancer goes out. Lum Kee puts his book down, takes his hat from the closet, and goes out.

The girl at the telephone is now talking about hats, while Nora fidgets with increasing impatience.

In his room, Robert is finishing packing a bag, with occasional glances at the bathroom that connects his room with Selma's. He does not make much noise but is still too drunk to be completely silent. He has changed his clothes.

Selma turns in bed and makes a faint moaning noise, but does not open her eyes.

In another room a bedside light goes on, and Aunt Katherine sits up in bed, listening. Grim-faced, she unhurriedly gets out of bed and reaches for her slippers.

His bag packed, Robert puts it out in the hall, then turns out the lights and tiptoes through the connecting bathroom into Selma's room, going to a dressing table, pulling a drawer open, and taking out a jewel case. He has transferred part of its contents to his pocket when Selma suddenly sits up in bed and screams, "Robert!" He turns, pushing the case back into the drawer as she snaps on the light.

Robert, with taunting mildness: "Hello, Selma, how are you?"

She runs toward him, crying: "Oh, where have you been? Oh, why do you do these things?"

He takes her in his arms: "There, there, darling."

For a moment she relaxes in his arms, then she puts her hands on his chest, pushes herself free, and cries, "No, I won't this time. I won't forgive you. I won't let you make a fool of me again."

Robert, as if to an unreasonable child: "All right, all right, darling. As a matter of fact, I only stopped in for a minute, anyhow, to change my clothes."

Selma: "Where are you going?"

Robert: "A trip, a little trip."

Selma: "You're not. I won't have it. I won't."

Robert, smiling: "Oh, won't you?" He takes a step toward the door, then stops to ask, "Want to kiss me good-bye?" She flies at him in insane rage. He catches her wrists, kisses her lightly on the mouth, says,

"Thanks, darling," releases her wrists, and goes out. She stands staring after him with wild eyes, scrubbing her lips with the back of one hand, then runs into his room and pulls a table drawer open.

FLASHES:
Robert, smiling, bag in hand, going out the front door into the foggy street.

Polly, standing in a small store doorway, straining her eyes trying to see through the fog.

Phil, at the entrance of a narrow alley, his collar up, his right hand under his coat near his left armpit.

Dancer, at the wheel of a black coupe, his eyes searching the street.

Lum Kee in a car driven by a Chinese chauffeur.

On a street corner, a policeman is hunkered down on his heels scratching the back of a gaunt alley cat. He hears a pistol shot (not too loud), straightens up, and starts across the street.

Robert lies on his back on the sidewalk, his head and one shoulder propped up a little by the wall he has fallen against—dead. Selma stands looking down at him. Her face is a blank, dazed mask. In her right hand, hanging down at her side, is a pistol. Brakes scream, and a car comes to a jarring halt at the curb. She does not move. David jumps out of the car and runs over to her, exclaiming, "Selma!" She does not move until he turns her to face him, and even then her face does not change. He shakes her, cries, "Selma! What—" He sees the pistol then and takes it from her, stepping back a little. As he does so, her eyes lose their blankness, and she looks at the pistol.

In a monotone she says, "He was going away. I took that from his room, to try to stop him." She begins to tremble, and her face works convulsively; she is about to go to pieces.

David has put the pistol in his pocket. He glances quickly up and down the foggy street, then takes her by the shoulders and shakes her again, putting his face close to hers, speaking very clearly, as if to one who understood English poorly, "Listen, Selma. You're going back in the house. You never had a pistol. Hear me? You haven't been out of the house. Understand? You know nothing about this. Understand?" She nods woodenly. With an arm around her, he leads her quickly to the corner, only a few steps away. There he says, "Now hurry! Back in the house. Up to your room. You know nothing about this. Run!" Automatically obeying his command, she runs blindly back toward her front door. David dashes back to his car, jumps in, and drives off with reckless speed.

In the Lichee, the girl at the telephone is now talking about shoes. Besides Nora, half-a-dozen other people are waiting to use the phone. Nora goes up to the girl and says, "Please, it's awfully important that I—"

The girl, dropping another nickel into the slot: "I can't help it if there's only one phone here. Why don't you carry around one of them portable shortwave sets if you got so many important things to call people about." She goes on with her phone conversation.

Nora goes back to Nick, who is engaged in rearing on his table one of those old-fashioned towers of bottles, salt shakers, oranges, forks, etc., all carefully balanced atop each other. Waiters and customers stand around with bated breath, watching him admiringly. He is getting along fine until Nora comes up and says, "Nick!" Then the whole pile comes crashing down on the table. The audience applauds.

Nick bows, then turns to Nora and says, "The divorce is Wednesday." She doesn't laugh.

Nora: "Nick, I can't get to the phone. One of the hatcheck girls has been talking for hours."

Nick: "You've come to the right place. Old Find-a-phone Nick, the boys around the drugstore used to call me." He offers her his arm, and they go across the floor and out of the restaurant. As they pass the pay phone, where the hatcheck girl is now talking about underwear and a dozen customers are angrily waiting, Nick says loftily, "Mere amateur phone-finding!" He opens a door, shakes his head, and shuts it. He starts to open the next door, but stops when he sees it is labeled "Ladies." The third door opens into Dancer's apartment. He bows Nora in, ushers her to the sofa, hands her the book Lum Kee had been reading, goes to the phone, and calls Selma's number.

The door opens and Dancer, in hat and coat, comes in.

Nick: "Hello, Dancer. Nice men's room you have." He waves a hand to indicate the room and the rather elaborate bath that can be seen through an open door, then suddenly frowns at Nora and asks, "What are *you* doing in here?"

Dancer stands inside the open door, looking at Nick with cold eyes, and when he speaks his voice is cold and level, "Once a gumheel always a gumheel, huh? I don't like gumheels, but I thought you'd quit it when you married a pot of money and—"

Nora, indignantly: "Did he call me a pot?"

Nick pays no attention to either of them; Aunt Katherine is on the other end of the wire. She says, "You'd better come over, Nicholas. Robert has been killed."

Nick's expression does not change as he says, "I will," and slowly hangs up.

Dancer, jerking a thumb at the open door behind him: "Well, now, if you're through in here."

Nick, leaning back comfortably in his chair: "Still foggy out?"

Dancer, very deliberately: "Have you ever been thrown out of a place, Mr. Charles?"

Nick, to Nora: "How many places was it up to yesterday, Mrs. Charles?"

Nora: "How many places have you been in, Mr. Charles?"

Dancer: "Look here!"

Nick, raising a hand: "Wait, wait! As I was about to say, it's not for me to tell any man how to run his business—though I *could* give you a few hints—but just the same it doesn't look right for you and your partner and your chief entertainer and one of your best customers all to go out at about the same time. It gives the place a—a—a quite vacant look. Did you notice it, Mrs. Charles?"

Nora: "Oh, decidedly, Mr. Charles. Quite barn-like."

Nick: "Thank you, Mrs. Charles. Now there's another thing. If Mr. Robert Landis came here with a lady who left a cigarette case, you shouldn't have sent it to his *wife*. You know what a fellow Mr. Landis was."

Dancer: "That wasn't me. Lum didn't know."

Nora leans towards Nick, her face strained: "Did you say *was?*" Nick nods slowly, his face serious now.

Nora, softly: "Poor Selma."

Dancer, angrily: "I've had enough of this. I—" He breaks off as through the open door comes the sound of Polly's singing.

Nick: "Ah! Another of our travelers has returned. Now if only—No sooner said than done," he says as Lum Kee comes in. Nick looks from one to the other of them and says thoughtfully, "I wonder which of you would be most frightened if Robert Landis walked in now." Neither man says anything. Nick: "But *you* know there's no chance of that, don't you, Dancer?"

Dancer: "I don't know what you're talking about, and I don't care." He advances threateningly. "Get out!"

Nick smiles, shakes his head: "You said that before, and it's foolish. We're not going to get out. We're going to have more people come in." He picks up the phone.

Dancer, grabbing at the phone: "Give me that phone!"

Nick: "Certainly."

He raps Dancer on the jaw with it. Dancer staggers back, holding his jaw.

Nora, proud of Nick, says to Dancer: "See?"

Nick dials a number, says: "Nick Charles speaking. I want to get hold of Lieutenant Abrams of the homicide detail. If he's not on duty, will you give me his residence number?"

Lum Kee crosses to the closet and carefully puts his hat away.

On a dark and seemingly deserted part of the waterfront, David gets out of his car, walks to the edge of a small pier, and throws Selma's pistol as far out into the water as he can.

Through the fog comes a man's voice shouting, "Hey, what are you doing there?" followed by the sound of feet running toward David. David races back to his car and drives off.

In Dancer's apartment, Nick is saying into the phone, "Sure, I'll wait for you, Abrams ... Well, I'll *ask* them to wait, but sometimes I think they don't like me well enough to do me favors ... Yes. I'll tell them." He puts down the phone and tells Lum Kee and Dancer, "The Lieutenant said something about boiling you in oil if you budged before he gets here. The fellow probably exaggerates."

Polly has finished her song. The sound of applause

comes through the door. Dancer turns on his heel and goes out.

A still larger and angrier group of customers is waiting to use the phone. The hatcheck girl is talking about pajamas. Dancer takes the receiver roughly from her and slams it on the hook, snarling, "Get back to work. What are you going to do? Spend the whole night here?" He goes on toward the restaurant.

In Dancer's apartment, Lum Kee says, "Dancer not mean anything, please, Mr. Charles. Good man—only excited. Sometime make a little trouble, not mean anything." He smiles cheerfully at Nick and Nora as if he had explained everything and says, "Now we have little drink, you bet you."

Nora rises, saying to Nick, "I ought to go to Selma's. She'll need somebody."

Nick: "Right. I'll put you in the car." To Lum Kee: "Hold everything." Nick and Nora go downstairs.

Harold is sound asleep now. The taxi driver is saying, "So I said to these two gobs, I said, 'Maybe you boys are tough stuff back on Uncle Sam's battlewagon, but you ain't there now,' I said. 'You're on land,' I said, 'and you're either gonna pay that fare or I'm going to take it out of your—' " He breaks off as Nick and Nora come to the car and opens the door for them. Harold wakes up.

As Nora gets in, Nick asks Harold: "Did you see Robert Landis leave?"

Harold: "No, I would've only—" He breaks off, leans past Nick to push the taxi driver violently with one hand, saying angrily to him, "Putting me to sleep with them yarns about where you told everybody to get off at! I ought to—" He jerks his cap off and turns to Nora, saying earnestly, "Aw, gee, I'm sorry, Mrs. Charles!"

Nick: "Did you see anybody you knew?"

Harold: "Nope, I didn't notice nobody coming out particular, except there was a kid come out right after you went in, and I only noticed him because he was kind of hanging around" (he indicates the doorway Phil stood in) "for a little while. Why? Something up?"

Nick: "What did the kid look like?"

Harold gives a rough description of Phil, adding, "Why?"

Nick: "What happened to him?"

Harold: "I don't know." He calls to the taxi driver, who is standing back against a wall, looking resentfully at them: "Hey, Screwy! What happened to the kid that was hanging around here?"

The taxi driver: "I don't know. I guess he went down the street half hour ago."

Harold warns Nick: "Maybe he never even seen him. What's up, Nick?"

Nick: "Plenty. Drive Mrs. Charles back to her Aunt's." Then to Nora: "Going to stay all night?"

Nora: "I think I ought to."

He nods: "I'll stop over in the morning." He stands at the curb, staring thoughtfully after the car as it drives away.

Upstairs in the Lichee, Dancer meets Polly as she leaves the floor and asks her, "What are you doing back here?"

Polly: "It wasn't my fault, Dancer. You know how drunks are. We got outside and he insisted on going home—his home—and I couldn't talk him out of it. I couldn't strong-arm him, could I? So I thought I'd better come back and tell you. I couldn't stop him."

Dancer: "OK, sister, dress your dolls the way you want to."

Polly: "I don't understand what you mean, Dancer."

Dancer: "A cluck, huh? All right. I'll tell you so you can understand. Somebody cooled off Landis tonight, and the heat's on plenty, right here. You're in it with me, and you're going to be in it with me, because the first time you step out of line—Get the idea?"

Polly: "You don't have to try to scare me." (But she is scared.) "I'm shooting square with you."

Dancer, sneering: "You mean starting now? That'll help some. Where's the paper?"

Polly: "In my bag. Shall I tear it up?"

Dancer: "Maybe you *are* as dumb as you act sometimes. Listen. Try to understand what I'm telling you. Landis is killed—dead. Maybe we're going to need that paper bad. So you don't let anything happen to it. Be sure you don't."

Polly: "All right, but I still don't get it. I don't know what you..."

Dancer: "Shut up and do what you're told."

At this point, as they move toward Dancer's apartment, they pass the head of the stairs and are joined by Nick, returning from the street.

Nick: "Now let's have that little drink Lum Kee was talking about."

Dancer: "Swell! And, Mr. Charles, I want to apologize for losing my temper like that."

Nick, linking arms with them: "Don't give it a second thought. Some people lose one thing, some lose another, but they all like a drink afterwards."

To Polly, sympathetically: "Tough you couldn't do a better job of seeing Landis got home all right."

Polly, sullenly: "It wasn't my fault. I did the best I could."

Nick, as they go into Dancer's apartment: "I'm sure you did."

Lum Kee is at the telephone, saying, "Better you come right away. You bet you." He hangs up, explaining blandly to Nick, "Mr. Caspar. He our lawyer. Sometimes good thing when you have trouble."

Nick: "You bet you."

Dancer: "Maybe, but I think you're going to a lot of trouble over nothing. It's a cinch none of us shot Landis, so what do we need a lawyer for?"

Nick: "Maybe to help you explain how you know he was *shot*."

Dancer: "Well, whatever way he was killed, it's still a cinch we didn't have anything to do with it."

Nick yawns, says, "A cinch is no defense in the eyes of the law," and makes himself comfortable on the sofa.

Dancer smiles ingratiatingly at Nick and says, "I don't blame you for thinking maybe we're tied up in this somehow. It's our own fault for starting off with you on the wrong foot, but . . . let's have that drink first and talk things over. We can show you we're in the clear." He pushes a button for a waiter.

Nick, indifferently, lying back and looking at the ceiling: "Don't worry about me. Talk it over with the police."

Dancer catches Polly's eye and jerks his head a little toward Nick. She nods and moves as if aimlessly over to the sofa. Lum Kee looks from Dancer to Polly, then goes over and sits on a chair not far from the sofa, but behind Nick.

Dancer calls, "Come in," as the waiter knocks and moves over so that he is between Nick and the door. (None of these movements should be definitely threatening, though it should seem to the audience that Nick is being surrounded.)

Dancer, to Nick: "What'll you have?"

Nick: "Scotch."

Polly and Lum Kee: "Same."

Dancer: "And a glass of milk."

The waiter goes out. Polly sits down on the sofa beside Nick and says, "Do you suppose that David Graham could have killed Robert?"

Nick blinks in surprise, then says: "I'm no good at supposing. What do *you* know about David Graham?"

Dancer is regarding the girl with a puzzled look.

Polly: "Only what Robert told me, that he was in love with his wife."

Abrams, stolidly: "Good evening, Mrs. Charles, or I guess it's good morning. Did you see him there? I mean Robert Landis."

Nora: "Yes."

Abrams: "What happened?"

Nora: "Nick knows. Go down there. He can tell you everything."

Abrams, not very hopefully: "I hope somebody can tell me something. These people!" He looks gloomily at Aunt Katherine and Kammer and shakes his head, then continues: "Anyhow, I got to ask a couple more questions. Dr. Kammer, do you often have to give Mrs. Landis things to quiet her?" Kammer stares at him. Abrams turns to Nora for sympathy, saying, "You see? That's the way it's been going."

Nora: "But surely you don't think Mrs. Landis . . ." She breaks off, looking from one to the other in amazement.

Abrams, patiently: "How do I know what to think if nobody'll tell me anything. Well, Dr. Kammer, let's put it plain: does she take dope?"

Aunt Katherine: "Mr. Abraham, you're insulting."

Kammer: "Certainly not."

Abrams, paying no attention to Aunt Katherine: "OK. Check that off. Then is she crazy?"

Kammer: "My dear sir, why should you think that?"

Abrams: "Easiest thing in the world. I've seen you three times in my life before this, and all three times you were on the witness stand testifying that somebody was nuts." He begins to count on his fingers. "First it was that guy Walter Dabney that killed a guy in a fight; then it was that Harrigan woman." He opens his eyes a little wider. "By golly, she shot her husband, too; and then it was ..."

Nora goes up to Abrams as if she were about to smack him and says angrily, "Too! What right have you to say a thing like that?"

Dr. Kammer bows to Aunt Katherine and says, "Miss Forrest, in view of this definite accusation by the gentleman" (He bows to Abrams) "I think you would be justified in insisting that your attorney be present at any further interviews members of your family may have with the police."

Aunt Katherine continues to regard Abrams in stony silence, as she has throughout this scene except for her one speech.

Abrams groans wearily and says, though not apologetically, "Anybody's tongue's liable to slip." Nobody says anything. He addresses Nora as if he were disappointed in her: "It's what you'd expect out of them, but you ought to know better." When she does not reply, he shrugs his shoulders and goes out.

Nora wheels to face Aunt Katherine and Kammer, asking, "Where's Selma?"

Aunt Katherine: "She's sleeping, my dear," adding quickly as Nora starts toward the door, "Don't disturb her. Dr. Kammer says she must not be disturbed."

Nora looks at them for a moment, then says very deliberately, "I won't disturb her, but I am going to be with her until she wakes up," brushes past them, and goes out of the room.

Aunt Katherine puts a hand on Kammer's arm and in almost a whisper asks, "Well?"

Kammer: "I think there is as yet no reason for alarm."

Nora goes into Selma's bedroom, where a dim nightlight is burning, and stands for a moment by the bed, looking down at Selma. When she turns away to take off her coat, one of Selma's eyes opens cautiously. Then she sits up in bed and whispers, "Nora!"

Nora runs to her, exclaiming, "But they told me you were..."

Selma: "I know." She unwads a handkerchief while she speaks, showing Nora two white tablets. "They gave me those to put me to sleep, but I didn't take them. I wanted to see you. I knew you'd come." Selma and Nora go into a clinch. Then Selma asks, "Has David come back yet?"

Nora: "I don't think so. He's not here now."

Selma: "Will you phone him for me, see if he's home?"

Nora: "Of course." She puts out a hand toward the bedside phone.

Selma, catching her arm: "No, not here. That's why I was afraid to phone. The police might be listening in. Go to a drugstore or something. Or, better, go to his apartment; it's only a few blocks."

Nora, puzzled: "But I don't understand."

Selma: "He took the pistol and told me to come

back and not say anything, and I want to know if he's all right."

Nora: "The pistol!"

Selma, rapidly, unconscious of the effect her words have had on Nora: "Yes. I took it and ran out after Robert when he said he was going away—you know, to scare him into not going—and he'd insulted me so terribly. And he turned the corner before I could catch up with him, and then there was a shot, and then when I turned the corner, there he was dead, and after a while David came and took the pistol and told me to come back home and not say anything to anybody. And now I don't know whether he's all right or . . ."

Nora: "Then you didn't shoot Robert?"

Selma, amazed: "Shoot Robert? Nora!"

Nora puts her arms around Selma: "Of course you didn't, darling. That was stupid of me."

Selma: "And you'll go find out about David? I was in such a daze or I wouldn't have let him do it; and I'm so afraid he may have got into trouble."

Nora: "I'll go right away."

Selma: "And you'll hurry back to tell me?"

Nora: "Yes, but do try to get some sleep."

Selma: "I will."

They kiss, and Nora goes out.

Nora goes softly downstairs and out of the house without seeing anybody, but as she hurries up the foggy street a man comes out of a dark doorway and follows her.

Aunt Katherine and Dr. Kammer are sitting in silence, as if waiting for something, when they hear the street door close behind Nora. In unison, they look at each other, then in the direction of Selma's room. Neither speaks. They rise together, and slowly—he dragging his lame leg, she leaning on her cane—they go to Selma's room. Selma lies as if sleeping. Kammer feels her pulse, then picks up her handkerchief and finds the tablets. He does not seem surprised. He pours a glass of water and says, not unkindly, "Come, why must you be so childish? Take these now." Selma, very sheepishly, sits up in bed and takes the tablets and water.

In David's apartment, he is distractedly walking up and down. He looks at his watch, goes to the telephone, but puts it down without calling a number. He lights a cigarette, puts it out immediately, goes to the window, then repeats his performance with watch and telephone. He is wiping his face with a handkerchief when the phone rings. He picks it up quickly. Nora, on the other end of the wire, says, "David, this is Nora. I'm downstairs. I want to—"

David: "Come up! Come up!" He goes to the door and waits impatiently for her.

As soon as Nora appears, David asks, "Have you come from her?"

Nora: "Yes. She—"

David, excitedly: "Where's Nick? What'll I do, Nora? It's my fault. I'm all to blame. If I hadn't given Robert those bonds, he wouldn't have been going away, and she wouldn't have"—his voice breaks and he almost whispers the last words—"shot him."

Nora: "But she didn't, David!"

David: "What? She told me."

Nora: "She told you what?"

David: "That she took the gun and ran out after him to try to keep him from going away and . . ."

Nora: "But she didn't shoot him. She hadn't turned the corner when she heard the shot, and when she got there he was already dead. She told me herself, and she was perfectly calm when she told me."

David sinks back into a chair, his eyes wide and horrified. He tries to speak twice before the words will come out, and when they do his voice is hoarse with anguish. "I've killed her, Nora! I've sent her to the gallows! I thought she shot him. I took the gun and threw it in the bay. I'm a fool, and I've killed her."

Nora, frightened, but trying to soothe him: "Perhaps it's not that bad, David. We'll see what Nick says. He'll know how to . . ."

David: "But don't you see? If I hadn't thrown the gun away, the fact that it hadn't been fired—and the police could've fired a bullet from it and seen that it didn't match the one he was killed with—don't you see?—it would have been absolute proof that she didn't do it. But now . . ." He breaks off and grabs one of Nora's hands, asking, "How is she? Do the police—do they think she . . . ? He seems unable to finish the question.

Nora: "Selma's all right. She's lying down. The police haven't talked to her yet. Dr. Kammer wouldn't let them."

David, a little sharply: "Kammer! Is he there?"
Nora nods. David, frowning: "I wish he'd stay away
from her." He shrugs off his thoughts about Kammer
and asks, "Do the police suspect her?"

Nora: "I'm afraid they suspect everybody."

David: "But her especially. Do they?"

Nora, hesitantly: "I'm afraid they do—a little."
Then, more cheerfully: "But they didn't know about
the Lichee Club and those people then. We were
there tonight and saw Robert, and Nick found out a
lot of things about Robert's running around with a
girl who lives in the same house as Pedro Dominges,
oh! a lot of things, and I'm sure by this time he
knows who killed Robert. So there's nothing to worry
about."

David, not sharing her cheerfulness: "I hope so. I'll
kill myself if . . ."

Nora, sharply: "Don't talk like that, David. They'll
find out who killed Robert; Nick'll find out."

David: "Tell me the truth, Nora. Does Nick think
she, Selma, killed him?"

Nora: "Oh, he knows she didn't. He knows . . ."
She breaks off, staring with frightened face past
David and pointing at the window. David turns in
time to catch a glimpse of Phil's face outside the window. He rushes to the window but has some trouble
with the fastening, so that by the time he gets it open,
the fire escape is empty. As he turns back to Nora, she
says in a surprised voice, "Why, that was . . ."

There is a sharp, triple knock on the door. David

goes to the door and opens it. The man who shadowed Nora from Selma's house is there. He asks, "Mr. Graham?"

David: "Yes."

The man takes a badge in a leather case from his left pants pocket and shows it to him briefly, saying, "Police."

Nora: "There was a man on the fire escape! The brother of that girl at the Lichee."

The policeman: "Yeah?" as if not believing her. He goes to the window and looks out for a moment, then turns back: "He's gone." Then he scowls at Nora and asks, "What girl at the Lichee?"

Nora: "Polly Byrnes, the girl Robert Landis went out with just before he was killed."

The policeman: "Say, you know a lot, don't you, sister? What does all this make you out to be?"

Nora, with great dignity: "I'm Mrs. Nick Charles!"

The policeman, apologetically: "I didn't know. I guess then maybe there was somebody on the fire escape."

Nora, indignantly: "Well, what are you going to do? Stand here and wait for them to come back?"

The policeman: "No, I reckon not." He goes to the phone.

David takes Nora out of the policeman's hearing and asks in a low voice, "Should I tell him about the gun, about Selma?"

Nora: "No, don't tell anybody until we see Nick."

[*To be continued in* NBM6.]

Action at Vicksburg

IRVIN FAUST

Irvin Faust has written six novels, including
Newsreel. *His most recent book is* The Year of
the Hot Jock and Other Stories. *Mr. Faust's
work is admired for its accuracy of speech and
detail, and he is an acknowledged master of the
New York prose style. He ranks "Action at Vicksburg" as one of his most successful stories. The
guidance head at a Long Island high school, Irvin
Faust lives in Manhattan and pays attention.*

THAT GENTLEMAN, Mr. Nagoya Ito, is from
the small but vital town of Matsumae, on
the northern island of Hokkaido, in the country that
his hosts often refer to as Nippon. He has been in
America for fifteen days, city-hopping from west to
east and traveling single-oh, which is by far the most
effective way to proceed. He has moved with speed

but with excellent care so that, with two days remaining, he has achieved the sensational megalopolis of the famous northeastern corridor. And so there he stands. Aiming his good, but not outrageous, camera, clicking, and briefly smiling. For his good, but not outrageous, telephoto lens has caught the first frame of what is surely the contradictory essence of this great and frustrating nation. Caught it at the perfect setting: the tomb of the most contradictory and essential general, United States Grant.

Click.

In those two shots Mr. Ito has caught the splendid combination of place and symbol, and no one, least of all the all-knowing expert, Mr. Kenzi Hayoko, who works beside him in the linen factory, can gainsay that fact. Mr. Ito has, indeed, in those shots, juxtaposed a magnificent and solemn resting place, containing a certifiable hero, beside a restless counterpoint that is known variably as Gotham, Baghdad-on-the-Subway, or most accurately, the greatest of Apples.

And something else . . .

As if to add an exclamation point to the proceedings, there we have a neat little plus. There, just on the top step of the Tomb. A small, sharp-boned Negro, who has cut himself out of the hallowed interior and is gazing at the roughness, the toughness, the coolness of the Apple.

Indeed, as luck, or Mr. Ito's pictorial instinct, would have it, the symbolic little chap is lounging quite innocently, in fact with a prototype nonchalance, beneath the beautiful words of the general: "LET US HAVE

PEACE." And hard by the rather bitter exclamation: "CRASH/SLASH/SMASH!"

To be quite blunt about it, the scene is delightfully heavy.

As he presses the camera button, Mr. Ito catches himself. "Negro," or even "colored man," as denoted within the Tomb, is out of fashion today; the chap in the doorway is a black man, or, simply, a black, and he must bear that in mind. For the excellent lens has zoomed up and is doing its work as well as ever, and from this careful distance on the wide approach, Mr. Ito can make out every carved-in line of the sad, dignified face, and that includes a scar that runs from beneath the left eye down to the firm but vulnerable chops.

Having recorded that map of wounded history, Mr. Ito moves to the other side of the walkway. He squints at his subject, who has turned and is gazing back to the dark mustiness of his liberating war. At that moment Mr. Ito's lengthy and careful research in Matsumae and Sapporo floods into his head: Mr. Catton's depictions of the struggle; the novels of C. Van Vechten who never met a "negro" he did not like; the recordings of Satchelmouth, of Cab, of the King, the Duke, the Count, and more recently the Prince; the lives of J. Johnson, J. Louis, and Ali the Great. All of that and much more run and gambol about the magnetic black, and as they do, there is another click, an internal one. For a name has entered the receptive head of the photographer-who-has-prepared.

Mr. Ito smiles to himself, quickly removes the smile.

But within his head, where research and practical experience interconnect, he continues to smile. Why not? The name born of that splendidly cool interconnection is perfect. As perfect as the face, the history, and the attitude of the little symbol.

Sugar.

Or, in moments of formality, Sugar Man.

It is an all-encompassing name. A proud and linking name. Reaching back to the stand-up geniuses of the prize ring, the double Sugars, Robinson and Leonard. But also a name that comments on itself, emerging as it does out of the native preoccupation with sweeteners, real and phony, and a name that captures another preoccupation, which quite frankly is money. As in bread, as in dough. As in Sugar. Click.

Mr. Ito (casually) swivels away. One must not be too obvious. There are other scenes that should flesh out the series, that can give it existential pizzazz. Thus he frames and snaps the Hudson as it rushes down to the sea, the very waters that carried Sugar's forebears here in the infamous middle passage, the very waters that carried here the forebears of the general who saved him. He also snaps tall, stiff New Jersey, gazing wistfully at pulsating Gotham. He moves slowly back to the walkway and focuses on a chunky man in a yellow and blue polo shirt. There is chunkiness all over, but it is especially pronounced in the lower gut, where it bulges out like a basketball. Another research click: the man is the perfect incarnation of the Cab Calloway chap, the one who measures five feet in all directions, or quite simply, one of those big, fat, solid boys, solid avoirdupois.

There is something else about the man. He wears a face of smiling weariness. Mr. Ito has seen a great deal of that face, as if its owner were hugely annoyed with his lot but has decided after many years of experience to treat it with a rueful disdain. The face, the corpus, are worth three pictures.

And then the camera swings to Sugar.

He is walking down the steps of the general's tomb. Ah. Once again, the sharp edge of interconnecting delight. This is turning into the best day since the morning in San Antonio when the Chicano lad smashed a bottle of beer against the Alamo.

Sugar is not merely walking; he is *limping*. Mr. Ito, not wishing in any way to embarrass his splendid subject, drops the camera to his right hip, glances expertly down, and snaps three versions of the limp. As he does, his busy and well-stocked mind zooms back to the little chap's early years. Hard, grinding years. Years, however, when he strode about strongly and smoothly. He had to, for he was one of twelve to fourteen children working the cotton fields of Alabama. Alongside sister B. McQueen; brother S. Life, who was constantly in difficulty with overseer B. Connor; and cousin K. Fish, who talked big but rarely acted. Sugar was a good worker, a hard worker, and he toiled behind his mask of pain from dawn until dark. But behind that neutral face lurked a brain, and in time that brain reached a dead-end conclusion. It decided that there was no future, no fulfillment, in such work. A parallel conclusion, by the way, to the one reached by Mr. Ito's grandfather in the copper mines of Wakkanai. All reached a climax on the day that the Northern Express came through and whistled, as it often did. However, this time the whistle was direct and quite personal, like the tales of Uncle Remus. Sugar looked up. Zip-a-dee-doo-dah. He found himself running. He found himself climbing. He found himself in a car with six other boys who introduced themselves as Scott. And they, and he, were on their way to a new world and a new life. Yes, a hard one, it is true, in the stone fields of the city, but one that gave you a chance to come smiling through. The way that Grandfather came through on leaving the mines. The way that the mighty Brown Bomber came through when he fled north to forge a new life against the anvil of the city of Mr. Ford, Mr. Chrysler, Mr. T. R. Cobb.

The scene has been inscribed. Mr. Ito leaps nimbly back to the present. He and his lens, still at his hip, track Sugar as he hobbles past the man who measures no more from head to toe than he does from side to side. Some ten feet beyond, Sugar stops. His powerful face is plunged into thought. Slowly he turns. Slowly he limps back to the man, stops. Well, now. They know each other. Right hands meet in the raised, slapping handshake. The greeting is recorded twice, now with the camera pressed against an eager cheekbone. The two men speak, and it is clear, even from a distance, that they are easy with each other. The jive spills out smoothly: change in the weather, change in the scene; difficulties with my wheels; worse difficulties with my chicks; R. Jackson unable to *purchase* a hit. And the raised hands keep slapping.

Mr. Ito pauses to reload, and as he does he considers. These two seem overly friendly. Even for Americans. Even for Rotarians. Even for a Van Vechten white exhibiting his rapport with a black. They really should not be this friendly.

Unless...

The film is inserted. Six shots ripple away beneath a happy finger. Mr. Hayoko had insisted that it was all Chinese propaganda, but here it is. All wool and many yards wide.

A transaction.

Clickclickclickclick.

With that fourth shot, Mr. Ito knows with a dead certainty who the fat man is. That is, given the circumstances that have brought the two of them here, who he must be. There are reels and pages of evidence: the Scarface, the Little Caesar, the Godfather. Lucky, Lepke, Baby Face, Mad Dog. Kid Twist, Bugsy, the French Connection. The round little fellow can be but one person: *The Dutchman.*

Dutch, to his friends.

No, not Arthur Flegenheimer, Mr. Ito is not that naive (for the King of Policy long ago bought the bloody bullet in that chophouse in Newark, New Jersey). Nor is he concerned any longer with numbers; times change and so does the big dough. This Dutch is playing the deadliest game in town, the Olympics of the Rackets. And playing it with the man who has been suckered from one misery to another. He is playing it with Sugar. A sigh, a click.

Mr. Ito thinks back to the lecture in Sapporo. The one that did not tell him anything startling but that made the scene a bit more graphic: "The Underculture of American Life." He thinks specifically of the film that was quite effective. In fact he shuddered several times during the film, even as he shudders now at the memory of *Reefer Madness*. But the shudder has added quality and depth to itself, for the two people in his viewfinder have clearly moved far beyond the dizzying weed. The deal they are involved in doing is the big time. The goods. The stuff. The merchandise.

He circles gently, keeping a good distance, and snaps various angles of the thrusting, climactic moment. He catches the smile of the Dutchman that has widened a millimeter, he catches Sugar's solemn mask. Catches a shake of two heads, professional nods, once more the stiffly perpendicular five. With a brief shock, Mr. Ito realizes that *this* is how they pass the merchandise. And he records three different perspectives of the expensive handclasp. In a short time, even the roughest and toughest frails will be kicking the gong around. Hardly a happy thought . . .

Dutch is looking at his hand. Still wearing the resigned smile with its touch of mirth, he is looking at his hand. Now, still with the smile in place, he is holding his hand out, palm upward. Sugar is examining the palm, like a gypsy reading fortunes. He is shrugging. Mr. Ito is pondering: open palm, shrug. Shrug. Ah. *Empty* palm. A palm sans merchandise.

Click. The Dutchman's smile hardens. Click. Sugar is gazing with an even defiance. Click.

Mr. Ito feels that it would be appropriate to turn away. This could be an extremely uncool moment. However, a socioeconomic problem has taken place and it must be captured if a realistic statement is to be valid. He places the problem in the center of his viewfinder and his finger descends. As it does, his active, reaching-out mind attempts to dig the ramifications . . .

It is quite clear that Sugar has not delivered the merchandise. Equally clear that somewhere soon the boss will be very disenchanted (Dutch, although powerful, is definitely not Mr. Big). When that chicken comes home to roost, the joint, to Sugar's detriment, will surely start jumping.

The camera, as Mr. Ito works out the scene, continues to pump smoothly away, a silent partner to its owner's busy, indeed teeming, brain. The camera catches Sugar talking very seriously and with great animation. No southern syrup here, no S. Fetchit, slipping and slurring. Now Sugar is pointing. The camera moves, catches the object of his intensity. The magnificent resting place of the hero general. Then it returns and catches Sugar plucking at the Dutchman's arm. It catches a suddenly bemused smile, catches Sugar talking even faster. In his lecture in the linen factory, the camera man will call this group "Yakking His Way Out of Trouble."

He frowns even as he takes the picture. That is most unfair. That hard-knock little man does not have to yak his way out of anything. He has paid a multitude of dues. If, on occasion, he has not always played on the straight and narrow, who has? Is the man pointing the camera so pure? Has he played flawless baseball? Mr. Ito flicks a shoulder; he is removing the image of the bosomy Rumanian woman in Beverly Hills, the evening of dice in Reno. He returns quickly to Sugar. He reaches for some more history . . .

There is the boy, attempting to improve himself in a school in the asphalt jungle. One can see him encountering hypocrisy, derision from his peers and, yes, from his teachers. They mock his dress, his speech, his manner. They cakewalk through the halls, dare Sambo to retaliate. He retains a firm grasp on his cool. Then on a climactic day it happens: the boy is conversing with the one person of empathic vibes, a golden-haired girl. One sees the bright face and the dark face talking with deep involvement at the top of a staircase. One sees white youths bursting into the scene, Rico, Tony, Alvin. The two are surrounded. Hard words. A blow. Another. A flaming rumble. The black lad falling heavily down the stairs, Rico giggling. The girl screaming. The boy's leg crumples beneath his still form. The others swagger off, the girl runs for help. The boy awakens in an emergency clinic; the Kildares can only do so much. The boy will never walk normally again. Or return to school again. Or forget again . . .

Mr. Ito stares through his powerful lens. The two men have stopped beating their unproductive gums. They have begun to walk. They are walking side by side, Sugar with a quickstep limp, Dutch with a long, rolling gait, as if he were running rum and the boat was heaving beneath him. They are heading for the steps of the Tomb. Zoom. Snap. But this is quite confusing. When a deal falls through, the Little Caesar should be furious. At the very least, highly indignant, for a huge amount of lettuce is involved. Instead, the two are strolling calmly into the quiet building. Is it possible that they will do their expensive thing *there?*

Mr. Ito saunters after them. Of course he lags well behind. They mount the steps and disappear beneath "LET US HAVE PEACE." He follows slowly, steps into the gloomy interior. Then, as if the general himself had nudged him, specific insight occurs. Sugar, quite simply, will not pass the goods under the very eyes of the man who smashed his chains! He has said this with very great emphasis so that the Dutchman cannot fail to dig the jive. He has, in addition, prevailed on his bemused partner to walk inside so that motivations will be perfectly clear. Acknowledging to himself that he may have sold Dutch a bit short, Mr. Ito mounts the steps.

In the quiet dimness the two of them are leaning over the marble rail. Sugar is pointing down. Dutch is nodding quite pleasantly. Holding his coolness at the ready, Mr. Ito strolls to the other side of the rotunda and then he also leans on the rail. However, he keeps an eye on his target: two gentlemen socializing, soaking up a bit of history.

They gaze down at the hero and his wife. The sepia member of the team is talking quietly and pointing down at the white caskets. The rise and fall of his voice is animated, but his face is especially sad. Small wonder. One has to infer that he has known only gold diggers and Minnie-the-Moochers in his checkered career. Frails who could not possibly have provided the affection and loyalty he needed, that Julia Grant gave to her better half. He has clearly struck a sensitive nerve, for Dutch is nodding heavily: he has had his own roll call of faithless molls. Mr. Ito zooms down and captures the singular devotion of the couple joined for all time. Very gently, he steps into the nearby alcove and records the long list of victories of the man who had nothing but support and encouragement in the home (he will enlarge this "fidelity" series and present it to Mrs. Ito). With a quiet sigh, he leaves the alcove.

They are gone.

They are not on the front steps.

They are not on the broad walkway.

Has Sugar flapped his excited gums in vain? Was Dutch oozing soft soap? Did he invoke the threat of the mob? Are some of the boys slinking about?

Mr. Ito quickly circles the Tomb, barely glancing at the scribbled tributes to Angel, Cheech, Batrat 80. Ah. There. Close by the iron-railed (rather insignificant) tribute to the general given by the Chinese many moons ago. He continues walking, with his tourist's mug, to a point some thirty yards beyond the pair. Deliberately then he turns, he focuses.

They are still peppering the atmosphere with their jive. But the give and take is no longer cool and smooth. They have obviously shifted into bitterness. He presses off five shots of the bitterness; it could mean trouble in River City for Sugar, but frankly, Mr. Ito is rather pleased. The little man has held to the high ground, he is clinging to his well-earned points. In fact, he is dishing it out with panache.

Experiencing a surge of elation, Mr. Ito swings around for some background material. He locates the calmly stolid International House, soaring Riverside Church. To his left a couple with the look of young American Gothic stamped on their open faces: Iowa, Kansas, Nebraska, Rocky Mountain high. He ripples off eight versions of Heartland Innocence. As he does he is aware, once more, of the voices of the "businessmen." They have jumped beyond bitterness. Bark. Snap. Dart. Crack. Back and forth, a bit like his son and best friend after a baseball game. Dutch is surely responding to the earnest little man: So you're on the level, so you're giving it to me absolutely straight, *so what?*

Sugar tells him so what, but is now getting it back in spades. As they harshly kick it around, Mr. Ito picks out one word. Over and over that same word. No, not a word. A name. Vic. Yes, Vic. The heartland couple are posing for a stranger, and Mr. Ito ponders Vic. Could he be Mr. Big? Is he the power behind that fat little throne? His ears focus as sharply as his camera. Vic. Again. Yet again. Chiefly from Sugar. He is certainly a major factor in his life, this Vic. Here we go again. Hold it, time out. Try another entry point. But of course. Mr. Ito gently tosses a smile at the

Gothics, but of course does not look at them. Our man is not Vic, he is *Vicksburg*. The town of Vic(k). And Sugar is digging up all the information planted long ago by the general, imparting same to Mr. Savvy. And surely throwing in some Sugar-history as an extra-added attraction. All of it adding up to the major point, and if my record is stuck in this groove, you had better believe it. I cannot pull a bad scene before the Hero of Vicksburg, under the gaze, if you will, of my main man.

Mr. Ito is itching to smile broadly. But he merely points his camera at the innocent couple, and then behind them, on the wall, at the rather nasty observation that "USA SIK."

The two men are walking again. Sugar heavily, Dutch with the smooth, rolling stride. He is also all action as he walks, arms flailing, waving away the classic siege on the Mississippi, gums flapping as if they were chomping air. No doubt he is asking the limping little man, "But what has your soldier boy done for you recently?"

Although his point has been missed by a country mile, Sugar is patient. The man brought me here, he gave me my chance. Remaining well behind, Mr. Ito clicks, nods.

They stop. Mr. Ito slides to one side, he stops. Sugar is pointing. To his feet. Cheap, worn-out canal boats. Now he points south, along the Hudson. Splendid chap. There is another river, Big Muddy. Sugar will make a pilgrimage down to Vicksburg on the banks of

Big Muddy. The loyal finger jabs thrice; along the way its owner will pay some overdue respects to Orchard Knob, Lookout Mountain, The Wilderness. Mr. Ito sighs with pleasure; the Pentax clicks with pleasure.

Dutch views it from quite another angle. One can easily dig his words; the context provides the content: "How do you make it to Old Man River in the absence of dough? And where do you obtain the dough if you do not do a deal?"

It is actually a very good point. Two good points. Shrewd points. From a very shrewd apple. They seem to tip the little man galley west. But only for a moment. He is responding and one does not have to be a mind reader: "Do not let it bug you. Where there is a will, there is a payday."

Very good. Excellent. The face of Dutch reveals that with utmost clarity. He is clearly wigged.

Sugar shrugs easily. He has a very skilled shrug. A bit like the shrug of Mr. Ito's son, but, of course, with much more sincerity. The two men gaze at each other. The camera gazes at the two men.

A break in the silent action. Dutch. Suddenly laughing. The laughter is building, then it is doubling over. Dutch is bending down, pounding the area above the fat basketball, searching for breath. Mr. Ito, frowning, snaps "Plump Hilarity." He remains with his subject, as finally, still gasping, he straightens up. Now that he is flying right, he points at the Tomb. He leans forward, and a word kicks out. It can be but one word: *Jerk.*

The camera swivels. The dignified face absorbs the word, not for the first time. Sugar is surely, and patiently, replying (and not for the first time), "Oh? Why a jerk?"

Expensive Bally shoes inch closer. Mr. Ito knows the answer to that one. He would dearly like to intercept the words, but the recording realist takes the picture, he does not paint it. He does, however zoom to his closest limit for the inevitable response:

"You are a jerk, old friend, because your winner is a *loser*."

The little man bears up beautifully. His words are soft, low, almost melodic. He wants to know the rationale behind that miserable jive.

The man who seems to be inflating under his cabana shirt comes back with the utmost coolness: "Because, my friend, your general was a rummy boozer."

Sighing, Mr. Ito swings to the general's bodyguard, his soulguard. If only he could answer as Cab Calloway would. Ah, he is answering. Oh yes, exactly like the Cab: "Hi-dee-hi-dee-hi-dee-hi!"

Dutch shakes his head sadly.

"Ho-dee-ho-dee-ho-dee-ho!" (Thank you, Cab.)

"I will say it again, old pal. He was a *bottle* baby."

Sugar is absolutely ready. "As President Lincoln remarked, not inaptly, 'Determine his brand of hooch and serve it up to my other boys.'" Sugar cracks a smile. "Take a quart for yourself, old pal." Four joyful clicks.

The man who had been in charge hesitates. The

Little Caesar is racking that cunning gray matter. Of course he will come back with something, the overseers always do. And, on cue, here it is, as Mr. Ito runs his sound track:

"All right, Sugar, I am heartily sick of this jive. I demand a full deck." Mr. Ito cranes forward. "Are you really and truly telling me you refuse to do a deal?"

The head of Sugar Man: a curt nod. "You have got it, old friend."

"All because of your hooching general?"

"Because of my general."

The grim smile narrows. "I suppose I can place that in my pipe and smoke it?"

"That would be cool."

"I dig . . . I dig . . ." The Pentax is jammed against its owner's cheekbone, but the finger on the button is pressing smoothly. The receiving mind is finely tuned:

"Sugar, you are pushing hard. So pay attention and dig me good."

Shrug.

"Hobba hobba good."

Shrug.

"All right, come and get it. Your general, you silly chump, was a crook, a low-down, dirty crook."

A tiny flick of the shoulder, as if the shrug is trying to fight through. Then the shoulder is quiet.

Dutch keeps going: "Well? What is your story, morning glory?"

The camera does not waver, it dare not. If only the

little man would reenter the ball park. Something, anything . . . Ah . . . Quietly, calmly: "President Lincoln said he was my man . . ."

Dutch eats that up, gobbles it up. "There is evidence, old boy, that President Lincoln did not always place both oars in the water."

"Hey, Dutch, don't say that."

"No? Play this on your record machine. Your general was the worst president we ever had. Double zero."

Suddenly, the sad, neutral face begins to sway from side to side, as if it were weaving away from tough, snapping jabs. Mr. Ito sends help, so does the camera, but the face keeps swaying, for the Dutchman is implacable:

"Look it up, check it out, shoot the liquor to me, John Boy. Your General made Warren G. Harding look like Little Bo Peep."

The powerful face is almost doing a loop-the-loop. And it is shrinking and wrinkled and twisted to one side. This is, frankly, quite difficult to observe, even though hugely sensational. It will surely produce a bark of admiration from Mr. Hayoko, and Mr. Ito clicks off six versions of the face to be absolutely certain.

Suddenly the equation changes. Sugar does the changing, the way the Sugar Rays came off the ropes. Swinging.

Face and head calm, controlled, he steps in swiftly on his one good leg, and quite amazingly and efficiently, on the little cat feet of Mr. Sandburg. As he does so he reaches into his back pocket. Dutch stares, then blinks, a crack in the smooth dike. But like so many of his class, he is only momentarily nonplussed; the heavy side of the equation does not readily throw in the towel in his world.

With extremely impressive dexterity, Dutch slides to his left, and with the same movement darts a hand into his shirt above the bulging basketball. His hand comes out of the shirt with a small, black object firmly cradled. In the following instant Mr. Ito hears a sharp sound, like a hard clap after a concert or a home run. And now Sugar is gazing at his erstwhile associate with some measure of surprise. Now he is clutching his right shoulder.

The picture is dutifully snapped, but even as it is, Sugar flicks a hand out to Dutch. A shining hand. No, correction, something shining *in* the hand. And now it is Dutch's turn. He is staring, really quite stupidly for a man with so many smarts, at his right forearm. But in all fairness, with due cause. The arm is turning as red as a New Jersey sunset, and, like the sunset, the red reaches to the ground. Ah, is *dripping* to the ground.

The heartland couple have received a genuine kick in the pants. They scream. They spin about and run, hunched over, across the street, toward the sheltering arms of the International House. Click.

Back to the action.

Sugar. He also spins. With surprising skill and alacrity, despite the bad leg, or because he has learned so well how to live with it, he takes an extremely exciting powder. The flap on his heels is a great help, but so is his keenly developed coping ability. While the camera records the flight, he dashes down the incline to Riverside Drive. Dashes across the Drive. Once Sugar is safely there, Mr. Ito turns with great coolness to Dutch. He raises the camera and zooms into a mug that makes L. Lepke look like Little Bo Peep. With terrific speed, emotion replaces emotion, and astonishment, disgust, bitterness possess the face that finally hardens into neutral resolve. Mr. Ito captures that decisive moment and then finds himself framing a raised, pointing arm and hand. He suddenly hears a voice: "Danger, danger, take care." He realizes, with a tiny jolt, that it is *his* voice. And that it is too little, too late. For he again hears the clapping sound, and, as Sugar glances back—a basic error, for when you split, you split—as he glances back, he clutches behind the knee of his good leg. Filled with gameness, however, he turns and hobbles south on the sidewalk.

Mr. Ito is focusing on the red, dripping arm and on the neutral, unblinking face above it. The small, black rod seems to be touching his camera, but of course it is the excellent lens doing its job. Mr. Ito snaps, suddenly wises up. He ducks and darts down the incline, and as he does he hears the clap, a *zinnnng* over his head. Perhaps he does not have wings on his heels, but soon he, too, is across the Drive.

He straightens up, looks south. Ah, there, grasping the back of the good leg. Sugar. Run-hopping along the busy sidewalk that curves beside the Drive and swoops down into the park. Mr. Ito follows with cool quickness, weaving through the strollers and joggers who are somewhat perturbed by the excitement in their midst but do not make it a federal deal.

Sliding the camera into its case, zipping the case, Mr. Ito glances across the Drive. The Dutchman, a genuine bulldog, has started, albeit heavily, down the incline. Unzip the case, get the picture? No. When in doubt, bug out.

Excusing himself, Mr. Ito continues to weave through the natives until he reaches the steps that dip into the park. He veers to his right and starts down.

As he skims easily along the sweeping curve, he presses the camera case to his side and briefly thanks President Fukashu for requiring daily physical education in the linen factory. Breathing properly, from the diaphragm, he feels quite strong, with excellent reserves of power, which, instead of overtime, may be called into play for grimmer purposes. In and out he glides, like a jitterbug cutting a slippery rug, avoiding the stream of people who are ascending and descending in their own matinee dance. Down, down, chasing after the principled little fellow who must by now resemble Mr. L. Diamond minus the Legs.

He finds him. Sitting against a tree, near a sharply eroded hill that at its bottom runs into the busy highway. Beyond the highway, the great river laps with complete neutrality at its stone banks. Mr. Ito kneels down.

"Can you move?"

With hugely dilated eyes, Sugar Man slowly shakes his head.

"Would you care to try?"

Once again he shakes his head, slowly, heavily. Then, with equal slowness and heaviness, he opens his mouth. His throat begins to work. The process seems incredibly difficult, and it occurs to Mr. Ito that he might well be observing a bucket being kicked. Well, then, at such a time it is vital to keep the patient in touch with worldly matters.

"Would you know," Mr. Ito says, "who is currently stomping at the Savoy?"

Sugar Man sighs. His eyes flutter. Ah, finally some reaction. Mr. Ito leans forward.

"Frip . . . Mama . . . never . . . *Vic* . . ."

Mr. Ito sits back on his haunches. Gently he thrusts the Savoy to one side. He considers. Yes, Sugar has kept his faith. He smiles. "Who can tell?" he says. "Perhaps one day you will get there."

"Whafor . . . never . . . Vic . . ."

"At the moment it does seem difficult," Mr. Ito agrees. "Perhaps if you attempt more optimism . . ."

"Ah frammit . . ."

"Frame it?"

"Frammit . . ."

"Of course . . . Are you quite certain?"

Breathing heavily, Sugar whispers, "Goddam frammit . . ."

"Yes, certainly."

Mr. Ito removes the camera from its case. He rises to one knee, frames the little man against the river, focuses, snaps. Sugar smiles weakly, the camera is replaced. Mr. Ito resumes the kneeling position. Sugar's head moves slowly, as if it were filled with lead; he gazes downriver. Is he searching for the tough guys of the Waterfront? Mr. J. Friendly, with his thick, foul cigar? No. Softly, he is rasping, "Leekum . . ."

"Leekum?" Mr. Ito says.

"Leekum . . ."

Mr. Ito ponders. "Lincoln?" he says.

Sigh. "Leekum . . ."

"Ah," Mr. Ito says. "Lee come?"

Briefly, Sugar closes his eyes, then opens them halfway.

Mr. Ito touches his shoulder. "Do not fear." He shakes his head firmly. "Lee does not come."

Another sigh, the eyes flutter. He seems composed, but his breathing is quite shallow. "I really must assist you," Mr. Ito says. Receiving no response, he reaches over and attempts to lift the little man. He is amazingly heavy. Mr. Ito eases him softly back to the reclining position against the tree. The eyes flutter shut. Mr. Ito feels a shock of alarm. He stands, looks about. Some forty yards to his left he sees a splash of green-topped tennis courts. Players of all shapes and colors are prancing, darting, plunging over the surface. However, beside a small brick house, near the closest court, a group is lounging, chatting, observing. "Excuse me," Mr. Ito says and rises and runs to a point several feet from the wounded man. He jumps up and down in the classic side-straddle-hop and waves his arms.

"First aid. First aid. Sick man. Require help."

Finally, at the sixth repetition, several in the group of four turn and observe him. He continues to jump, shout, wave. They converse with each other. They come to a decision. They walk toward Mr. Ito and Sugar Man. With a sense of accomplishment, Mr. Ito turns back to the little man who is looking extremely weary. And now the group of four joins him. A man, a woman, a teenaged boy, a girl who might be classified as an emergent adolescent. Mr. Ito points to the man on the ground.

With a sharp moan, worthy of Miss V. Mayo noting an expiring J. Cagney, the woman kneels beside Sugar. The man also kneels. He seems knowledgeable, for he feels for a pulse and checks his wristwatch. The preteen girl stares upriver. The boy bounces his racquet against the heel of his hand and says, "We'll miss our turn."

The woman, to Mr. Ito's great satisfaction, ignores the lad. The man, having finished with Sugar's pulse, such as it is, unwraps his belt and straps it tightly about the bleeding leg above the knee, noting that "This may hurt, old man."

Sugar nods as if he understands, and the V. Mayo woman smiles at him. Much of her hair, Mr. Ito notices, could pass for a shade quite close to gold. He steps back, for the two of them seem to be in competent control. At that moment Sugar glances up at him and surely mouths "Vic." Mr. Ito smiles; he nods. Very well, a change in plan, but a necessary one. Tomorrow he will board a bus and travel south. To Orchard Knob, to Lookout Mountain. To The Wilderness. To Vicksburg. And if he encounters the likes of Messrs. J. Blue Eyes, C. Lucky, or M. Dimples, he will invoke the code of *omerta*. Looking down, he guarantees that the canary has never been a favored bird of the Ito family. He nods again, crisply. Sugar rests his reassured eyes.

The man turns to the boy. "Go back, tell Carlos to phone the police for an ambulance."

"Are you serious?" the boy replies. "We'll never get a court."

The woman is about to round on him when the man shouts, *"Don't argue with me, Chip."*

Chip clearly takes the same vitamins as Mr. Ito's son. He remains in place and shouts back with equal vigor.

Mr. Ito sighs and looks away from the group. His eyes follow the curving staircase. At the top, looking around while others stream past, is a brightly shirted figure with a straining gut. His left hand reaches across his chest and holds onto a dangling arm. Now the man takes a halting step down, as if testing the firmness of the stone. Quickly, deftly, Mr. Ito removes his Pentax from the case and reloads. He removes the telephoto lens that has performed so faithfully and screws in a wide-angle replacement. He snaps the man, who, like his namesake in the blood-soaked Palace Chophouse in Newark, New Jersey, refuses to throw in his towel, even though his companions, Mr. L. Rosenkrantz and Mr. A. Berman, have kicked a vicious bucket. The mug may not be admirable, but he is tenacious.

Someone else is tenacious. He is lying there in his green pasture. The all-important question is: Are the angels shouting "Gangway! Gangway for de Lawd God Jehovah!" Wait. His hand moves, his eyes twitch. He may be communing with de Lawd; he has not yet joined him. Mr. Ito feels quite elated; if the great Puzo himself were to pump him for information, he would come away with a pail of clams.

In the meanwhile, the group of four do their specific things: The second Miss Mayo dabs at the shoulder of Sugar with her hat. The man shouts at the boy, the boy shouts at the man. The blossoming girl gazes raptly at the George Washington Bridge.

At the same time, the tennis players, with varying degrees of skill, are swarming and lunging about the courts. Joggers skim by, in particular, a blade-thin female who is making for the steps down which the Dutchman is wobbling as he clutches the dripping arm.

Mr. Ito circles to a point at the lip of the drop-off that leads to the highway and thence the river. He sinks easily to one knee and aims his wide-angle lens at "An Urban Landscape, with Incident."

He replaces the camera. Carefully he zips up the case. With calm strides he walks to the foot of the steps. He stops. So has the Dutchman stopped. Dutch has, by far, seen palmier days. The intent female jogger brushes past him and continues up the stairway. Others veer around the two of them; they are like an island in the sun. They look at each other. The Dutchman is swaying, as if he were listening to the Savoy in his head. His eyes are not quite focused. But a wounded lion is a twice-dangerous lion. It is absolutely essential to stall for time if Sugar's chances are to be thicker than urine on a rock. Mr. Ito is prepared. He rifles through the research cards in his mindfile. He swiftly decides: Like the venom of a snake, he will use the Dutchman to counteract the Dutchman.

Reaching back to the mortally wounded Flegenheimer, mewling on his hospital bed, Mr. Ito firmly proclaims, "A boy has never wept, nor dashed a thousand kim."

Aha, the man before him focuses. He stares.

"Mother," Mr. Ito assures him, "is the best bet, and do not let Satan draw you too fast."

Well, now, he is blinking. Mr. Ito notes with pleasure that he no longer carries any heat. Mr. Ito glances past him and up. At the top of the stone steps blue uniforms are gathering, and their heat is at the ready. Obviously the heartlanders have replaced their starch; when the going got tough, their toughness got going! The blue uniforms start down.

Mr. Ito looks back over his shoulder. The wide-angle tableau remains more or less the same, except that now Miss V. Mayo is dabbing with her sock and Sugar is sporting the semblance of a smile; he may be punching with powder puffs, but he is still punching. Mr. Ito turns back to his adversary who is swaying in a long, thin circle. The Little Caesar, at such a moment, said, "Mother of God, is this the end of Rico?" Dutch merely keeps swaying and staring.

Mr. Ito grants the flash card in his mind a silent thank you. Thank you, Arthur Flegenheimer, you have been of enormous help, but you are free now to cash your own ticket. As for Mr. Dewey and Senator Kefauver, one trusts that you are not too displeased with this day's work. However, Nagoya Ito would prefer to take it from here.

The Dutchman is beginning to sag at the knees. His eyes are fanning quite rapidly, but he is paying very careful attention as Mr. Ito thrusts out his hand and says with brusque animation,

"Well, twirl my turban, man alive, can *this* be Mister Five by Five?"

Shopping Cart Howard

JAMES LEE SNYDER

James Lee Snyder has been writing for fifteen years, but "Shopping Cart Howard" is the first story he has sent out for publication because, as he puts it, "I wanted to refine my work first. . . . Now, on good days, I feel like I have complete control of my writing."

"Shopping Cart Howard" is an amalgam of two or three people Mr. Snyder knows. "Living in New Orleans, you are exposed to a broad range of people and experiences," he observed. Though a private detective has a prominent role in the story, it is not about crime and thus would not normally be included in NBM. But we felt the rules should be stretched in this case.

DICK TRACY's been following me for days. I know it's him because of those awful, baggy suits he wears and the way he acts, a real funny-paper hero, this one. He slides in and out of doorways and window-shops enough for ten country wives come to town. Brother. So what I do is I take him down to the Quarter, down on Bourbon Street and him always a block behind, and I park him in front of one of those male strip joints down there. Then I'm rearranging my cart for an hour or so while the tourist jerkers slither out and work him over. It's pitiful what those leech bastards can do to you with that much time. Once, Dick just up and left. They all started calling him Peeping Tom and a couple of the boys came out in their wigs and nighties, running their fingers beneath that official Dick Tracy hat, and he vamoosed. Now the last couple of days he doesn't follow me in. He waits on Canal, has a Coke at Woolworth's lunch counter, and I pick him up on my way out. I've about decided he's actually with the Internal Revenue. They must have heard about all that money I was making, not paying taxes on, and sent him down. Duke and Reese might have tipped them off. They're convinced I have a buried treasure somewhere, and it would be just like those fools to ask the government for help, if they thought it would do any good.

Of course, he may be with one of those social houses. Some loafer on the state payroll or, even worse, one of those goddamn Jesuits in disguise. Brother Marti's been trying to get me to stop by and partake a free lunch for years. It breaks his heart to see me managing out on the street all by myself. He likes to walk among his herd at meal times, all those street jerks kissing his behind while cramming down his baloney and Wonder Bread sandwiches. He turns into Jesus once he passes out the cellophane-wrapped sweet rolls. Everybody falls to their knees and prays, then he runs them back outside so they can line up again. Pitiful.

You see, the Brothers and the welfare people think I'm crazy, and I let them. It enhances my freedom of movement. They're always stopping me here and there to "inquire" about my well being. That's when I sort of roll my eyes around in my head—go all trancelike, I mean—and try to run them over. I'll chase them down the street with my cart while they're begging me to let them give me a hand. I sure hope Dick's not one of them. That would destroy all my romantic notions about him.

I've come to decide it's my unique lifestyle that gives them their opinions about me. Ever since I drifted into New Orleans, ten years or more ago, I've lived out on the street. Well, a few days during the cold snaps I'll go into some boardinghouse, but it's right back out after that. The difference is I'm always clean and neat. I see filth, under most any circumstances, as inexcusable. Twice a week, Wednesdays and Saturdays, I go over to the Y on Lee Circle and pay a buck twenty-five for a hot one. First time I did so, just after hitting town, the clerk grilled me about it. Did I not have access to bathing facilities elsewhere? "Plumbing's broke," I told him. "I'm on the landlady now, but she's old and moves like a caterpillar." After a while they took me for granted and didn't say a word. Then a few years later, when the old clerk was quitting, he introduced me to the new fellow and explained the situation. "Plumbing's down at home," he said. "The landlady's very old and slow." "Slow as a caterpillar," I backed him.

After Saturday's scrubdown I drop by this washerteria on Prytania and do my laundry. I always maintain three sets of khakis. That gives me a clean one after each bath. Then every other month I'll have my old felt slouch cleaned and blocked, and I'm ready. The point is it's not hard to maintain yourself, unless you're just plain lazy.

Another sore point with those that have is my manner of doing business. I'm into metals recovery, scrap aluminum over to the recycling plant on Tchoupitoulas, and my particular approach just kills Brother Marti. He's a shuddering, red-eyed mountain of fat every time he swigs down one of his ever-present Coca Colas and tries to hand me the empty bottle, and I refuse. You see, other street jerks go for a dime wherever, garbage cans, gutters, phone booths. I don't just mean cans and bottles, but also old batteries, rags, newspapers, hubcups, tires, you name it; and none of them, of course, are beneath panhandling or just plain begging for that night's dew. They all have that wandering, hungry look about them that sets them apart. Animal desperation that Marti loves.

Not me.

"I only do cans," I tell him, while that pudgy hand's extended, just praying I go for the wooden nickel. "That's aluminum—bagged and ready to go."

Just *kills* him.

See—getting here, I go around to all these businesses, bars, restaurants, warehouses, even some of the big office boys downtown, and I tell them my story. I'm neat and polite, and it's usually not too hard to get them signed up. Then I always leave a brand-new garbage bag, tie wrap included, and tell them what their pickup date will be. I kind of make them feel wanted—that old hometown milk-route atmosphere—and it works like a charm. People stop me going by now, really wishing they could be on the list too, and I have to turn them down. "Filled up, sorry," I tell them. Then I'll take out my note pad and jot down their names "just in case." I've got a whole page of hopefuls.

I push around this old Winn-Dixie "We're The Beef People!" shopping cart. Now don't think I stole the damn thing. I found it over near the expressway, all beat up and a wheel missing. A little colored boy sold me an original Dixie caster for fifty cents (he had a whole display case to choose from), and I oiled and cleaned the whole thing up like new. Now it's kind of famous around town. "Here comes Shopping Cart Howard," all the old bags holler out the windows of their shotguns. I don't mind too much. Though it does have a senile sound to it that gets under my skin. Brother Marti tells me I should return it to its rightful owner. "Then you might make yourself a nice wooden one," he advises. I consider pushing that heavy-ass board tank all over the place and give him my crazy eye-rolling routine, and he drops the subject.

Dick Tracy's closing in. With Duke and Reese, that makes three hot on my trail. Now the motivation of those two neighborhood brands is as obvious as hogs in a sweet potato patch. They know my operation and want their share, or the whole damn thing. Not so Dick. He's asking questions around, and it's got me puzzled. I normally take my noon meal at the Lovebug Grill on Rampart Street. I go in, and Leroy Henderson sets down a steaming plate of red beans and rice, two juice-popping sausages, and a cup of chicoried jake alongside that's one of life's joys and wonders. Now Leroy tells me some "weird, funny-talkin' dude" has been around inquiring. It's Dick, of course, and he's asking all about me. Wants to know my name and anything about my background. Wants to know about my family, and Leroy, black as bituminous coal, informs him he's my one and only brother, which sends Dick packing.

"He fuzzy," Leroy tells me. "But he ain't off no local peach."

"Where from?" I ask, shoving in the beans.

"Nawth, maybe," says Leroy. "He sound all bullshit jive—don't talk no sent-zes. Just dis n' dat—like Kojak."

"Or Dick Tracy," I add.

"Who dat?" Leroy inquires.

Now I find he's been asking around elsewhere, talking to my customers along the route. Of course I can't have that, because it makes some people nervous, and business is just that. Then, I consider my past and the reasons for the way things are my business. I prefer to have people think I've been a rustic, bearded old coot forever. It makes things simple, and if there is one thing I've sought my last twenty or so years of roaming about, it's simplicity.

So what I do is I begin to stalk Dick Tracy.

I find him over on the corner of Camp and St. Joseph, talking with none other than Duke and Reese. Now this crossroads happens to be one of the great hobo gathering places, not only of New Orleans, but of the entire world. And Dick's polyester pinstripes stick out more than ever.

I come up behind him and say, "Listen, Dick, I'd like to ask you to stop bothering my customers."

He turns around, his hawk face all gagging surprised, and nearly swallows the Lucky Strike dangling between those thin, cruel lips. "Nail it, canman," he says, and walks away with his own personal fifty-mile-an-hour arctic tail wind pushing him along.

"Listen, Shoppin' Cot," says Duke, grinning, "whut choo done now?"

"Robbed the Poydras Whitney," I reply and start getting out of there myself.

Reese, a scrawny, pock-faced white, as opposed to Duke's sprawling jungle blackness, hisses, "Save it, you old geek. What are you doing down at Western Union each month? You send money out, don't you! Don't you! Listen—"

By now, I'm vamoosed.

After that, odd enough, Dick's a little more open about things. The elusive atmosphere dwindles; that is, his sneaky ratlike demeanor calms somewhat. I find that regretful, but it's easier on the both of us. For whatever reason, he has to trudge after me all over the city, I accept it, and it becomes something of a routine. I have nothing to hide, and I finally begin to enjoy our little game. Dick, it seems, has a job to do, and I've never been one to interfere with any poor soul's livelihood.

So we strike up sort of an unspoken agreement, and it's fine after that. Dick doesn't have to duck foolishly down any more alleyways, and I don't have to keep worrying about losing him in the crowd, because a tailsman he's not. From dawn to dusk he stays close. He comes to know my pattern so well, he can drop out at any moment, say, into a bar for a cool one, then merely check his watch and head across town to catch up with me. He walks only a short distance behind me now. He smokes, chews gum, and maintains his expression of utter boredom. After introductions, my customers also greet him, which he openly resents, but, being such a prominent part of my day, I begin to worry about his feeling left out. We eat together at Lovebug's counter, although he always makes sure there's a couple of stools between us. One day I buy him lunch, and the next day, resentfully, he returns the favor, with Leroy telling me, "Kojak say tighten up, canman."

"Just being hospitable," I turn to him and say. He ignores me and busies himself looking through the toothpick jar for a clean one.

Saturday nights, as is my routine, we go to the movies. For years I've gone to this Cuban picture show up on Magazine. They show all the old stuff up there, double-feature westerns and adventures and coppers, which I enjoy. Of course everything's in Spanish which, initially, I see drives Dick crazy. That first time, with Don "Red" Berry up there babbling away, he sort of looks over at me and shakes his head. But after that he loosens up. The following week is Gable night and, believe me, you can hardly get a seat because of it. The first one's a real rough-and-ready and, halfway through, I glance over and see Dick cheering things on with the rest of them. He's sharing his popcorn, and they're all slapping him on the back like one of the boys. During intermission I find him talking pidgin English at the candy counter, buying everyone Snickers and cold drinks, then back inside they go.

After the show a funny thing happens. Dick saunters over and says, "Cuppa jake, canman?"

"Why not," I reply. I figure this is the big moment, anyway, so I say, "Let's go back to my place."

Which shocks the hell out of Dick. He's using his little finger to pick corn kernels out of his teeth when he hesitates, then catches himself and blends it real nice. "Machts nichts, canman." Of course I'm confused with myself, then realize I've had enough and want to get everything out in the open where I can see it. The truth is no one knows where I live. Not a soul. Dick knows that from asking around and reacts accordingly. Oh, he's tried to follow me home often, but I would just get him down into the warehouse district, which I know like mom's face, and cut him loose. One night Duke and Reese were tagging along too, and it was a regular night at Mardi Gras. I stayed on the streets an hour longer than usual because I was having so much fun. And the real killer was, just as I was ready to do my Harry Houdini, this crummy Camp Street special floats by, pushing his cart. Now, it wasn't nearly the same, but I guess the three after me were too tired to see that, and, I'll tell you, it was a sight to behold. There he headed up River Road, which just winds on and on forever, and those three right after him. Dick didn't show up for a day or so and was sore as hell because of it.

But now I've got a feeling about him. I don't know who he is or why he's doing this, but I don't think he means me any harm. And, if he did, I would just pack up and move on, because, like I've said, I stay real close to the ground.

So I take him over beneath the big New Orleans bridge and show him my compound. It's tall Cyclone fencing, and we slip in through this rear corner. Inside is a lot of weeds and bushes, and right in the middle is my camp. What it is, is this stack of oil-well pipe. There are a dozen sections and they're huge, each one about three feet across. I imagine by now anyone's forgotten it's even here, because, as I've said, I've never had any visitors.

With the street lighting nearby there's a continuous mercury vapor glow over everything, and Dick takes his time looking around. Meanwhile, I fire up the Coleman and get our coffee ready.

"Bedroom, canman?" Dick asks, peering into one section of pipe. My folded linen and accessories are within.

"I move around," I tell him. "Get bored with one hole and move on to the next."

Dick finds my little fluorescent camplight and clicks it on. Then he's rummaging through my book box, reading the titles. He finally pulls out one of my port bottles. "I figured you hit it," he says with a sneer.

"Old habits," I reply. "When I was, shall I say, respectable, evenings I would sit back in my recliner with some cold Jack London and warm ruby. It was pleasant."

We sit there on a couple of cinder blocks, and Dick insists we have the port with our coffee. Then, afterward, we just sip on the wine, passing the bottle back and forth. Dick's smoking one Lucky after another, and I don't say a word. Soon he's had enough and blurts out, "Canman, you're something else."

"What do you mean, Dick?"

"Name's Blue," he comes back. "Bob Blue."

"Like Dick better."

"Don't care too much for Howard myself, canman."

I nod and say, "All right then, what's the scoop?"

And that's when he hands it across, and I'm just floored. It's a letter, you see, from my sister Alice. Haven't seen her since I took off, around twenty-two years ago. I was thumbing my way out of town the day the first Kennedy boy was murdered.

"You're working for Alice?"

He motions for me to read the letter. Which is not the easiest thing for me to accomplish, but I do so.

Dear Howard,

   May I introduce to you Mr. Robert Blue, a private investigator from San Francisco. Now

139

I know he's a little "different," but a few others I contacted did not seem interested in my proposal, while Mr. Blue seemed genuinely excited about it. Anyway, he said he'd never been to New Orleans and would like to see it. Howard, I asked Mr. Blue to locate you and see if you would return with him to stay with me. Now before you throw this letter back at him, let me have my word, and I will not consider doing this again. That is all I ask, my darling brother.

Now you've been sending me money about every month. For some reason you must have thought I needed it, but that's not the case. I still have my art dealership and do very well with it, although I've cut back some on my workload. Howard, Harry died of a heart attack a few years ago, and the poor old bum's insurance money would have easily seen my retirement, if that was my desire, so you see the situation. I've just been taking that "poor sister" dough you've sent me and banked it. There's about forty-seven thousand dollars in there, last time I peeked, which is enough change for anyone's fishing trip.

I've left you alone till now, Howard, because I knew that's what you wanted. After your phone call, about 1965, I believe, I knew you had to run it out. Each of us deals with tragedy their own way, and you had that right. Honey, I've gone to bed every night these twenty-two years wondering what you're up to. That, you see, was one of the things I asked Mr. Blue to do. I wanted to know, once and for all, what you were up to now. Whether you were happy and safe or what. After that he was to approach you with this letter or get the hell away from you. So, if you're reading this, he has called me and I've told him to see you.

Simply, I think you've taken this far enough, Howard. I've been more than fair with my side, and I expect you to think about that. We're not young now, and honest to God I need you around before I get out of here. We're all there is, you know. There may be a cousin or so tucked somewhere, but I don't count that. I love you and want you with me while there's time. If you're married again, which I doubt, we can all have a wonderful time together. I live up in the valley now. It's some wooded property, and there is the main house and a smaller guest place. You're welcome to either one, although I prefer you stayed in the larger house with me. It's quiet, Howard, and lovely. You know the valley.

Not much else to say. I love you, and if you decide to stay there, you have your reasons, but I doubt I would agree. You know I would not hamper your life in any manner. I only want you back again. Enough is enough.

Love,
Alice

After this I'm contemplating the ground before me very hard. I tell Dick, "I thought she was on welfare. Someone I ran into told me that. Or that she filed bankruptcy. I can't remember exactly."

Dick's cracking open a Lucky and shaking his head. "No stories today, Mr. Greenjeans. You wake up one morning and think you're the Invisible Man: poof— El Splits-o. Couple of birthdays later your sister gets this phone call, collect, mind you, from Windy City."

"It was dead of winter, Dick," I say without reason.

"It was breakfast time in sunny California," he says. "Sis and hubby are eating their corn flakes, minding their own, when suddenly the horn blows, and she's hearing some old sot crying about the good old days, singing 'The Way We Were,' and how can he make it up now."

For a while I'm speechless, trying to understand what's going on. I'm remembering that phone call and say, "I was thinking then about when we were kids, her and I; us playing together, then being older and her going away to the institute, then her coming home and being delighted with my little winery and family and my leased Ford station wagon."

"Charming," says Dick, yawning and blowing smoke at the same time. He was different, all right. "Reminiscing with a rummy at daybreak must have been just peaches and cream for her. But let's talk about now. Like the letter says, canman, she needs you, not your score note a month and a question mark."

Then I'm shaking my head. "You're wasting your time."

"I get it," he says. "You'd rather turn into Grandpa Prunes one day and wax line one of your stovepipes over there."

"What's in it for you?" I snap back. "I suppose, I go back, you get yourself a nice bonus?"

He was smiling, dangling that Lucky. "Ditto. I get five more Cs on my report card if I bring you back alive—but not kicking."

"Well I damn sure would be," I say. "She knows I could never do that again. Damn her, anyway."

"Easy, Howard, I promised sis I'd leave my shotgun home." He stands up now, stretching and looking around. "Anyway, your pet rats are getting on my nerves. What say we beat it for a quick nightcap?"

"Sorry, I'm limiting my social drinking these days."

"One for the road," he says. "Tomorrow I fly the friendly skies."

"Is that right?" I reply. For some reason, this news bothers me. In any event, after hearing this I have to agree, and we end up at this seaman's bar over by the river, which I know all the way there is a mistake. We have a drink, then two or three more, and I'm starting to tell Dick how it happened. Luckily, he stops me. I hadn't talked about it for a while, but, as I should have known, it never did leave me in the best of spirits. Talking about it, that is.

So Dick's blowing smoke, raising his hand and saying, "Save it, old-timer, sis gave me all the painful details before I left."

By then I am feeling pretty rude and say, "Oh, yeah?

What the hell does she know about it? What makes
her so damn smart?"

Dick's eyeing me real close now through those half-
closed eyes of his. I hear him say, "Your problem is
you've got a case of the sorries for yourself you've never
been able to shake."

"Go to hell," I reply.

"No, I'm going over to the Monteleone and go to
bed," he says. "I've got a full tank trying to figure out
why such a nice lady as that wants an old coot like
you hanging around."

Then he just disappears and there I am alone again.
I start feeling guilty about it after a while, what I'd
said and the way I'd acted. It was Dick still working
on me. He was so damn sure of things, which made it
even worse. Miserable puritan.

"Get you anything?"

It was just the bartender and me left. "Oh, hell," I
say. "A big cup of the blackest, meanest coffee you
got."

After he sets it down, he hangs around and we talk.
Soon I start feeling the pressure ease up inside me.
The beer jerker's telling me about a catfish farm he
wants to get going. It's the big dream of his life, so
we chew on it for fifteen minutes or so. Then he asks
me what I do and, all clear headed, I start telling him
about the winery. The one, I'm saying, I used to own.
The funny thing is, it is the first time I've talked about
it without being tight. For some time now I had
equated sobbing and drooling into my whiskey glass
with the running of a winery.

Now I am fresh and loose as sheets flapping in an autumn breeze in Maine.

I tell him carefully about how the thing used to run. I was recalling how much hard work and fun it had been, and I think he picked up on it. Then he asks me, if it was that good, why wasn't I still there? In former times this would have been the cue to pull all stops. I'd learned a hundred ways to milk sympathy from some stranger, and the details of my personal tragedy got them every time. And, at that moment, more by habit than intention, I almost do the same thing again. I open my mouth to speak and suddenly feel the notion disappear. Of course it's all still there. It's picture perfect within my mind: how my wife Mary and our two boys—Brad was four and Danny was six —had got up early one morning and gone down to the city shopping. My birthday was around then, and I think they were going to get a present for me. Then I'm over in my warehouse moving empty casks around when Harry (who was chief of police in town) comes up crying his eyes out. It seems this car had pulled across the highway in front of our car and everyone was dead. The other folks, I found out later, had been to an all-night wedding shindig and were on their way home. I remember I kept thinking how, just before it happened, everyone in both cars must have been happy. They must have been smiling and feeling very pleased about things in general. I recall it was a beautiful day.

But now I only look at the bartender and say, "Change of luck, I'm afraid. You know how that is."

He does and goes into familiar detail about some woman leaving him for another guy, and what he'd do if he ever ran into them. But I'm polite, letting him finish before I get the hell out of there.

The next thing I know I'm back at camp, but nothing looks right anymore. It's like, after bringing Dick around, nothing's the same anymore. So I leave again and just go walking. I end up at the Moonwalk, which is this elevated boardwalk overlooking the Mississippi. Behind me is Jackson Square and the Pontalbas, and, what I do is, I spend the rest of the night there. Just sit there and think. I recall how I'd moved in with Harry and Alice for a few days before I took off. I woke up one morning and felt short of breath. I sort of stumbled about the house, not being able to breathe properly. I was gone before Harry got up to start the coffee. Damn her, I was thinking now. *Damn* her.

In the morning I'm there watching the light appear around me. The ferries start crossing the river, and there's a mist hanging over the river and through Algiers. In the square behind me people are starting to come out. The pigeons are sitting on Andrew Jackson, ruffling their feathers and yawning. The French Quarter streets pull away in either direction. They look low and mean and very lovely in the gray mist. Now I'm seeing this motley little faubourg with all its cracks and humps and distortions, and I know it's not telling all of the truths about itself. That would be too painful, I guess. Its mask is affixed, and it wakes up each day and slowly stretches and doesn't say too

146

much about yesterday. Then there's the carts rolling in on their wooden wheels, and the rosy faces having breakfast over at Royal Orleans, and I know it's all right and I can lean back again.

Alice, I'm thinking, always had a good sense of timing and was always dangerous to be around for that reason. She encouraged you to do things where you knew damn well the odds were stacked against you. Like the time she talked Mary into going up in one of those gliders. Now high heels usually made my wife dizzy, but there she was one day, floating all over the valley, with her instructor before her and Alice in one right behind. Harry and I were sitting out on my patio having scotch and sodas when they went over. I couldn't believe it, but they sure enough tipped their wings before heading up-valley again. Harry and I laughed like birthday boys when that happened.

But that was Alice. She reminded me of Lucille Ball, except she kept the whipped cream in the can. I couldn't imagine her now, slowing down, but I could figure she still had something left. After all, she dug up Bob Blue and sent him to me. When that came to mind, I knew I suddenly wanted to talk to her about it. About all of it. It was a nice thought, us sitting out on the porch, chewing the fat. It was such a hell of a nice thought, all right. Talking with Alice again was a challenge that suddenly appealed to me. Seeing her again. I didn't see it as a question of having paid one's dues, but I knew this was the first thing I had really wanted to do in some time. It was not a routine mo-

147

tion. It was a quest. After that, it was only a matter of keeping my ass out of those gliders. I guessed she would have one tucked back somewhere.

So I call up Dick and tell him it's a go. There are a few things I have to do, I tell him. Want to turn over my route to Leo, who's this mildly retarded Quarter fellow I know. He scrounges cans but doesn't have the sense to organize. But this would be set up, and otherwise Leo is very professional. Then I have to pick up my things and say *adios* to a face or two.

"I'm going with you," says Dick.

"That's not necessary. I'll meet you at the hotel."

"Look, canman, you're sitting in my new Monte Carlo."

"Don't worry, I'll be there shortly." And I hang up on him and get busy. I spend an hour or two making the arrangements and doing my tidying up. Leo is pleased as hell with the offer and is hugging me and promising me the world he'll take care of my, or his, cart. Since Leo is one of the world's great amateur spray painters (always catching the can sales at Ben Franklin's), I picture something in translucent blue with wheels akin to Joan Crawford's lipstick. I hurry on, giving the nod to Brother Marti, and he holds out, one last time, that squatty little Coke bottle of his. And so I take it, thinking it may be the appropriate memento to my time down under.

Back at camp, things are not so cheerful. Duke and Reese are there, having made a thorough inspection of the place and my possessions and evidently not finding what they came after. They've finished off my final bottle of port, and Duke is telling me how they saw me wandering around the night before and followed me back. I look around and say, "So what now?"

Reese spits and hisses his displeasure. "This is it, you old geek. You got money hid here somewheres. You sold enough cans to go to fucking Panama. Where's it at?"

"Mailed it off to my sister," I tell him. "You know I do, Reese. You've seen me."

"*All* of it?"

"All but necessities. I've got some pocket money you can have."

"You sumbitch," says Duke. "We don't want no raggedy-ass dime 'n nickel. We want dem *dollahs.* Say, Reese."

I stand there a moment, then make some idle comment about seeing what I can do for them. I start backing away when Reese lunges at me, and I take a swing at him with Brother Marti's bottle. It comes down a good one across his head, and he hollers out loud and curses me. Duke is there, and I feel the bottle knocked away while his big arms come around me. It suddenly feels like an Oldsmobile is parked across my chest and I can't breathe at all. Now they start dragging me off into the bushes with Reese hitting and kicking at me as we go. Then it crosses my mind about Alice, and I'm sorry, knowing she'll believe, for the rest of her days, that her timing was off on this one.

They got me in the bushes now, really giving me hell-for, when I hear this real smooth voice saying, "Table open?" It's Dick, you see, a fresh Lucky stuck between his lips and palming the prettiest nickle-plated .38 I think I've ever seen. Duke and Reese drop me like a wormy apple, with Reese going on about what right the other had sticking his nose in.

"I got six rights, pizza face," Dick tells him, then raises the revolver up to make his point. "You and your friend should really go play someplace else—like Kentucky."

I think that's a good one, even in my condition, and I enjoy watching the both of them back out of there. They hit the street at a brisk shuffle and disappear.

"You coming?" he asks, putting his gun away. "Or maybe you want to go play hopscotch on Canal Street?"

"All right, Dick," I finally say, letting him help me up. I'm sore as hell all over but can't help getting in the mood. "Let's make like a tree and leave."

"Ditto, canman."

We vamoose.

Rain in Pinton County

ROBERT SAMPSON

Robert Sampson may be best known to students of popular culture for Yesterday's Faces, a five-volume study of pulp magazines that is being published by Popular Press. Volumes one and two—Glory Figures (1983) and Strange Days (1984)—have appeared, and the next two volumes are with the printer. In addition to his scholarly work, Mr. Sampson, who is a management analyst at the Marshall Space Flight Center in Huntsville, Alabama, has published about two dozen mystery stories.

FAT RAINDROPS rapped circles across puddles the color of rusty iron. Ed Ralston, Special Assistant to the Sheriff, said, " 'Scuse me," and pushed through the rain-soaked farmers staring toward the house. Ducking under the yellow plastic strip—CRIME SCENE, KEEP OUT—that bordered the road, he followed the driveway up past a brown sedan, mud-splashed and marked "Sheriff's Patrol."

Behind him, a voice drawled, "He's her brother."

The house, painted dark green and white, sat fifty feet back from the county road. That road arced behind him across farmland to hills fringed darkly with pine. Black cattle peppered a distant field. The air was cold.

In the rear parking lot, a second patrol car sat beside a square white van with "Pinton County Emergency Squad" painted across the state outline of Alabama. On the shallow porch, a deputy in a black slicker watched rain beat into the yard.

Ralston said, "Punk day, Johnny. Fleming get here yet?"

The deputy shook his head. "They're still calling for him. Broucel's handling things inside." And, as the door opened, "I'm sure as hell sorry, Ed."

"Thanks."

He entered a narrow kitchen, went through it to a dark hallway that smelled faintly of dog, turned left into the front room. There a handful of men watched the photographers put away their gear.

When he entered the room, their voices hesitated and softened, as if a volume control had been touched. Men stepped forward, hands out, voices low: "Sorry. Sorry. Ed, I'm real sorry."

He crossed the familiar room, keeping to a wide plastic strip laid across the beige carpet. He shook hands with a little, narrow-faced man who looked as if he had missed a lot of meals. "Morning, Nick."

"Sorry as hell about this, Ed," Nick Broucel said.

Ralston nodded. His glasses had fogged, and he

began rubbing them with a piece of tissue that left white particles on the glass. Without the glasses, his eyes seemed too narrow, too widely separated for his long face. His dark hair was already receding. Scowling at the flecks on his glasses, he said, "Well, I guess I better look at her."

A gray blanket covered a figure stretched out by the fireplace. Ralston twitched back a corner, exposing a woman's calm face. Her hair was pale blond, her face long, her lipstick bright pink and smudged. On the bloodless skin, patches of eye and cheek makeup glared like plastic decals.

He looked down into the face without feeling anything. There was no connection between the painted thing under the blanket and his sister, Sue Ralston, who lived in his mind, undisciplined, sharp-tongued, merry.

He stripped back the blanket. She was elaborately dressed in an expensive blue outfit, earrings and necklace, heels; nails glittered on hands crossed under her breasts. "Well, now," he said at last. "It's Sue. What happened?"

Nick said, "She went over backward. Hit her head on the corner of the fireplace. Pure bad luck. Somebody moved her away. Smoothed her clothes. Folded her hands. Somebody surprised, I'd say."

"Somebody shoved her and she fell?"

"Could be."

"Or she just slipped."

"Could be."

Rain nibbled at the windows. The investigative

work had started now, and the room squirmed with men standing, bending, looking, methodically searching for any scrap of fact to account for that stillness under the gray blanket.

Ralston asked, "Why the full crew? How'd we hear about this?"

"Anonymous call. Male. Logged at 5:32 this morning. Gave route and box number. Said the bodies were here."

"Bodies? More than one?"

"Not so far." Broucel looked sour and ill at ease. "This is Fleming's job, not mine. I'm just marking time here. I don't know where the hell he's got to. Where's the sheriff?"

Ralston said carefully, "He's taking a couple of days vacation." He slowly scanned the room. Money had been freshly spent here, money not much controlled by taste. New blue brocade chairs bulked too large for the room. The couch seethed with flowered cushions. The lamps were fat glass creations with distorted shades. Tissues smeared with lipstick scattered a leather-topped coffee table.

"And there's something else," Broucel said.

He gestured toward the shelves flanking the fireplace. Cassettes of country music littered the bottom shelves. On upper shelves clustered carved wooden animals, ceramic pots, weed vases. Centered on the top shelf was the photograph of a grinning young man. It was inscribed "To Sue, With Ever More Love, Tommy."

"You recognize that kid?" Broucel asked.

"Isn't that Tommy Richardson? His daddy owns the south half of the county."

"That's the one."

"Daddy's going to enforce the dry laws, jail the bootleggers, clean up the Sheriff's Department—come elections. That's a mike, isn't it?"

"Yes, sir, that's a mike."

A fat wooden horse had tumbled from the second shelf. Its fall had exposed the black button of a microphone, the line vanishing back behind the shelves.

In a slow, reflective voice, Ralston said, "Sue never had a damn bit of sense."

"Let's go down in the basement," Broucel told him.

Steep wooden stairs took them to a cool room running the length of the house. Windows along the east foundation emitted pallid light. Behind the gas furnace, a small chair and table crowded against the wall and black cables snaked out of the ceiling to connect a silver-gray amplifier and cassette tape recorder. On the table, three cassette cases lay open and empty, like the transparent egg cases of insects.

Broucel said, "We found three mikes. About any place you cough upstairs, down it goes on tape."

Ralston gestured irritably at the equipment. "I don't understand this. She didn't think this way. She couldn't turn on the TV. Why this?"

Broucel fingered his mouth, said in a hesitant voice, "I sort of hoped you could help me out on that."

"I can't. I don't know. We didn't speak but once a year."

"Your own sister?"

"My own damnfool sister. She had no sense. But she had more sense than this."

"Somebody put this rig in. She had to know about it."

"Must have," Ralston agreed. "Must have. But what do I know? I'm no investigator. I'm a spoiled newspaper man. My job's explaining what the sheriff thought he said."

Feet hammered down the stairway. A deputy in a dripping slicker thumped into the basement, excitement patching his face red. He yelped, "Nick, we found Fleming."

Broucel snapped, "Where the hell's he . . ."

"He's in his car, quarter of a mile down the road. Tucked in behind the brush. Rittenhoff saw it. Fleming's shot right through the head."

Broucel sucked in his breath. He became a little more thin, a little more gray. "Dead?"

"Dead, yeah. He's getting stiff."

"Oh, my God," Broucel said. His mouth twitched. He put two fingers over his lips, as his eyes jerked around to Ralston.

Who said, with hard satisfaction, "I guess we're going to have to interrupt the sheriff's vacation."

He drove his blue Honda fast across twelve miles of back-county road. A thick gray sky, seamed with deeper gray and black, wallowed overhead. Thunder complained behind the pines.

He felt anger turn in him, an orange-red ball hot behind his ribs. Not anger about Sue. That part remained cold, sealed, separate. It's Piggott's doing, he thought. Piggott, Piggott, Piggott the beer runner and liquor trucker, the gambler, briber, the sheriff's poker-playing buddy. Now blackmailer. What else? And Sue's very particular good friend, thank you.

Whatever Piggott suggested, she would, bright-eyed, laughing, follow. No thought. No foresight. Do what you want today, ha ha. More fun again tomorrow.

When he last visited her, they had quarreled about Piggott.

"He's lots of fun," she said loudly. Her voice always rose with her temper. "He's interesting. He's different all the time. You never know with him."

"You always know. He'll always go for the crooked buck. He handles beer for six dry counties. He owns better than two hundred shot houses. He's broke heads all over the state. Even a blond lunatic knows better than to climb the sty to kiss the pig."

It ended in a shouting match. She told Piggott the next day, with quotations, and Piggott told Ralston and the sheriff the day after.

"A full-time liar and a postage-stamp Capone." Piggott pushed back in his leather chair and yelled with laughter. "I swear, Ed, I didn't know I was that good."

"Hardly good," Ralston said.

The sheriff's eyes, like frosted glass, glared silence.

Ralston said, "Look, Piggott, Sue's just a nice, empty-headed kid. She sees the fun, but she don't smell the dirt. She's got no sense of self-protection. She's different."

Piggott swabbed his laughing mouth with a handkerchief and straightened in his old leather chair. Amusement warmed his face. "I know she's different. I'm going to marry her, Ed."

The Honda reeled on the road. He jerked the wheel straight. It was not quite nine o'clock in the morning and cold, and the road twisted as complexly as his thoughts.

Two miles from the highway the fields smoothed out, bordered by white fencing that might have been transplanted from a Kentucky horse farm. When the fence reared to an elaborate entrance, he turned right along a crushed-gravel road gray with rain. A square, big house loomed sternly white behind evergreen and magnolia. In the parking lot, two Continentals and a dark green BMW sat like all the money in the world. Rain sprinkled his glasses. As he walked across the road to a porch set with frigid white ornamental-iron chairs, the front door swung open to meet him. A slight man with very light blue eyes and a chin like a knife point waved him in.

"Out early, Ed."

Ralston nodded. "I need the sheriff bad, Elmer."

"He just got to bed."

"Tough. Tell him it's official and urgent."

The man behind Elmer snorted and showed his teeth. "Official and urgent," he said, arrogantly contemptuous. He was thick-shouldered, heavy-bodied, round-faced, and scowled at Ralston with raw dislike.

Elmer said, "I can't promise. The game lasted all night. You and Buddy mind waiting here?"

He stepped quietly away down a high white hallway lined with mirrors and horse paintings. The hall, running the length of the house, was intercepted halfway by a broad staircase. Beyond lounged a man with a newspaper, his presence signifying that Piggott was in.

A sharp blow jarred his arm. He turned to see Buddy's cocked fist.

"We got time for a couple of rounds, Champ."

Ralston said, "Crap off."

Buddy, hunched over shuffling feet, punched again. "Ain't he bad this morning." Malice rose from him like visible fumes. "The sheriff's little champ's real bad. Couple of rounds do you good. You lucked out, that last time."

"You got a glass jaw," Ralston said.

Elmer appeared on the stairway to the second floor. He jerked his hand, called, "Come on up."

Ralston walked around Buddy, not looking at him. Buddy, clenching his hands, said distinctly, "You and me's going have a little talk, sometime."

The second floor was carpeted, dim, silent, expensive, and smelled sourly of cigars. Eddie pointed to a carved wooden door, said, "In there," wheeled back down the hall.

Ralston pushed open the door and looked at Tom Huber, Sheriff of Pinton County, sitting on an unmade bed. The sheriff wore a white cotton undershirt, tight over the hairy width of his chest, and vivid green and yellow undershorts. Hangover sallowed his face. He was a solid, hard-muscled old roughneck, with a hawk-nosed look of competence that had been worth eighty thousand votes in the last four elections.

He said, "Talk to me slow, son, I'm still drunk."

Easing the door shut, Ralston said, "Last night, Fleming was shot dead. In his own car. In the country. With his own gun, couple of inches from the right temple. Gun in car. Wiped off. Far as we know, he wasn't on duty. You need to show up out there. Broucel's in charge, and he's got the white shakes."

"Fleming shot?" A slow grin spread the sheriff's mouth. "So that grease-faced little potlicker went and got himself killed. That's not worth getting a man out of bed for. Let Broucel fumble it."

"Fleming was your chief deputy," Ralston said sharply. "You have to make a show. The media's going crawl all over this. You got to talk to the TV—sheriff swears vengeance. Hell, we got an election coming."

"There's that." The sheriff touched his eyes and shuddered. "Lord a mighty, I didn't hardly get to sleep. Cards went my way all night."

In a neutral tone, Ralston said, "You don't ever lose, playing at Piggott's."

"That's why I play at Piggott's." He got up carefully. "God, what a head. Well, now, that's one less candidate for the high office of Pinton County Sheriff. Ain't it a shame about poor old Lloyd Fleming?"

He moved heavily into the bathroom to slop water

on his head and guzzle from the faucet. Ralston drifted around the bedroom, face somber, peering about curiously, fingering the telephone, light fixtures, pictures.

The sheriff emerged, toweling his head. "I'm scrambling along, Ed. Don't prance around like a mare in heat."

Ralston said, "I need to tell you a little more. But I'll save it. Too many bugs here."

"I counted one," Huber said pleasantly.

"Two, anyhow." He knelt to reach under the airspace of a dresser and jerk. His fingers emerged holding a microphone button and line. It seemed a twin of the one on Sue's shelf. "These may be dummies to fake you off an open phone tap."

The sheriff sighed. "It's hard for an old fellow like me to bend over to squint in every hole. You know, you got to like Piggott. He don't trust nobody."

They returned unescorted to the first floor. "I best make my good-byes," the sheriff said. "Not fit for a guest to leave without he thanks his host for all those blessings."

Ralston followed him to the rear of the white hall. The watcher there, a burly youngster with a face like half a ham, stared at them eagerly. The sheriff asked, "Piggott up?"

"Oh, Lordy, sure," the youngster said. "He don't hardly ever sleep."

He clubbed the door with his fist, opened it, saying, "Mr. Piggott, it's the sheriff."

A cheerful voice bawled, "You tell him to bring himself right in here."

It was a narrow, bright room stretched long under a hammered-tin ceiling. The walls were crowded with filing cabinets and messy bookshelves, stuffed with as many papers and magazines as books. A worn carpet, the color of pecan shells, led to an ancient wooden table flanked by straight-backed wooden chairs. Behind the table, Piggott lolled in an old leather chair.

He bounced up as they entered. He burst around the table, vibrating with enthusiasm, grinning and loud. He had curly black hair over a smooth face, deeply sun-burned, and he looked intelligent and deeply pleased to see them. "Didn't expect you up till noon, Tom." He smiled brilliantly. "Lordy, you're tough."

He pounded joyously on the sheriff's shoulders, then seized Ed's arm. "Now you come over here and look at this picture. You'll like this."

He extended a large color photograph. Sue Ralston beamed from it. She stood close to Piggot, arms clutching each other, heads together, delighted with themselves.

Through rigid lips Ralston said, "Nice photo." He felt nauseated.

Piggott burst into his rolling laughter. "That's our engagement photo, Ed. Listen, don't look so sour." His arm slipped around Ralston's shoulders. "It's OK. I'll make a great husband. I grow on you."

Ralston swallowed, standing stiff within the embrace. "Piggott . . ."

" 's all right, Ed. I know." He smacked Ralston's

shoulder amiably. "It's a funny world. Who wants a postage-stamp Capone for a brother-in-law?"

He emitted a howl of joy, throwing back his head, opening the deep hollow of his mouth. "Even us booze merchants fall in love, Ed. We even get married. Ain't it a crime?"

Ralston forced, "Congratulations, then," from his closed throat. It was now imperative to tell them about Sue. But he could not. He listened to Piggott and the sheriff bantering. He could not.

Piggott had set it up, sometime, for some purpose. And she was dead because of it. Somehow. Set a trap and what dies in it is your responsibility.

"Fleming!" Piggott was saying. "I can't believe it. Who's Moneybucks Richardson going to run for sheriff now?"

Laughter. The sheriff edged toward the door.

The need to tell them about Sue, the urgency of it, tore at him. At the door, he blundered to a halt, said, "Piggott . . ." Terrible pressure locked his throat. He said, instead, "Piggott—what about that ancy-fancy recording stuff in Sue's basement?"

Fleeting hardness in Piggott's face softened to laughter. He flung out joyous arms. "Wasn't that something. We told some friends we were engaged. Then I went out to the car and let them warn her about me. Then we played the cassettes back to them. Funny! Hell, they'll never speak to me again. Hey, you got to hear those tapes. And they're my good friends."

Joy wrinkled his big face. He bellowed laughter like a furnace. "I mean, funny."

They sat in the sheriff's car behind Piggott's house. Rain rattled on the hood and glass.

Ed asked, "What are they doing with Tommy Richardson?"

"Son, you probably don't want to know anything about that."

"I got to. It's important." Their eyes met, held, strained, force against force. "Yes," Ralston said. "I mean it's important. It's important to me."

The sheriff shrugged. " 'Tain't but a trifle. They're just roping the boy a little. Just a little business insurance."

"Business insurance?"

"Why sure. Here's a nice respectable boy gaming around with beer runners. Well, shoot, people game and people have a drink now and then. Least I've known them to do it in Pinton County. Don't expect they'll change. No harm in it, less they get mean. The mean ones is what sheriffing is about. But you can't never tell when sin's going to get a bad name. So maybe Old Richardson goes and gets a hard-on against sin. Then they got something for him to listen to while he gets calm. Or maybe not. You can't ever know."

"That's all?"

"All there is. Nothing a'tall."

"Merciful God," Ralston said. "Is that all?"

He got out into the rain. He stood staring blankly, hunching up his shoulders, rain smearing his glasses, distorting the world so that it appeared twisted and in strange focus. He circled the car and tapped the sheriff's window, and rain ran in his hair, wet his forehead, ran from his chin.

The sheriff's window rolled down.

Ralston said, "Sheriff, Sue's dead. At home. Fell and hit her head. I couldn't tell Piggott."

He turned away and walked toward the front parking lot. The cement driveway danced with silver splashes.

Behind him, a car door slammed and heavy footsteps hurried back toward the house.

The Honda streaked toward Pintonville. He had, perhaps, a ten-, even fifteen-minute start on them. More if Piggott delayed. The road flew at him, glistening like the back of a wet serpent. Soon they too would think of questions to ask Tommy Richardson.

If it had been Tommy who was with Sue last night.

If he had read the evidence correctly.

If Sue had got herself up, polished and shining, to dazzle the son of Old Man Richardson, the fun and indiscretion funneling into the cassette's hollow maw.

If the boy had found the mike. If his suspicions blazed . . .

But Fleming. He could not understand Fleming's presence.

The Honda slid on the shining asphalt, and the back end fought to twist around. He corrected the wheel, iron-wristed, jabbed the accelerator.

First, talk to Tommy Richardson. Before Piggott.

The car leaped. The rain came down.

"I'm Tommy Richardson," the boy said in a low voice, affirming that being Tommy Richardson was futile and burdensome. His head drooped, his shoulders slumped, his body was lax with self-abasement.

"I'm Sue Ralston's brother Ed. I'm with the Sheriff's Department. I'd like to talk with you."

"I guess so." He pushed open the screen door separating them, exposing his consumed face. He was unshaven, uncombed, unwashed. He smelled of sweat and cigarettes, and despair had drawn his young face and glazed his eyes. "Dad says you guys are incompetent, but you got here quick enough."

He looked without hope past Ralston's shoulder at the rain sheeting viciously into the apartment complex. Lightning snapped and glared, blanching the pastel fronts of the apartments and rattling them with thunder. "Come in. You're getting soaked."

Ralston stepped into the front room, saturated trousers slopping against his legs. Tension bent his tall frame.

Stereo equipment, lines of LPs, neat rows of paperbacks packed the cream-colored walls. A table lamp spilled light across a card table holding a typewriter and a litter of typed pages, heavily corrected.

"I've been up all night," Richardson said. He gestured toward the typewriter. "Writing out my incredible . . . stupidity."

He turned away, reaching for a typed page. As he did so, Ralston saw, behind the boy's left ear, a vivid pink smudge of lipstick.

The room convulsed around him, as if the walls had clenched like a fist.

"Mr. Ralston?"

He became aware that Tommy was holding out typewritten pages to him, eyes anxious. "This explains it."

"Sit down," Ralston said.

"Thank you. Yes, I will." The boy collapsed loosely on a tan davenport, long legs sprawled, head back, eyes closed, hands turned palms uppermost, the sacrifice at the altar. On the wall behind, two fencing foils crossed above the emblem of the university team.

Tommy added, without emphasis, "I thought really serious things were more formal. You expect personal tragedy to have dignity and form. But it doesn't. It's only caused by trivialities—stupid mistakes, misjudgments. Nothing of weight. All accident." He might have been whispering prayers before sleep.

Ralston, set-faced, read:

CONFESSION
of
Thomas Raleigh Richardson

I am a murderer.

Last night, I murdered two people that I cared for.

One I loved and loved deeply. The other was my friend. But it was wholly by capricious and accidental chance, which now seems inescapable, that I murdered both of them. That it was essentially accidental does not excuse me.

167

The balance of the paragraph was crossed out. There were four pages, scarred by revision, ending with his full signature.

Ralston took out his pen and laid the pages in Tommy's lap. "Sign your usual signature diagonally across each page." He watched, immobile, as the boy wrote. Then he folded the sheets and thrust them into his breast pocket.

"Now tell me what happened," he said.

"I loved her. We were planning to get engaged. At first I thought she was a criminal with Piggott. But she was sensitive and warm. You're her brother. You know. She didn't know about Piggott, what he did. We fell in love. We were going to get engaged after I graduated."

"How did you get involved with Piggott?" Ralston asked. The tremor shaking his legs and body was not reflected in his voice.

"It was Fleming. Dad had a Citizen's Committee for Law and Order meeting at the house. Fleming came. He said that the sheriff and the bootleggers were cooperating. But he needed more evidence. He said that Piggott would try to blackmail me to make it seem like I was participating in his business. He called it a business. Dad didn't like it, but he agreed that I would let them try to blackmail me."

"So then Fleming introduced you to Sue."

"I met her at his house. Twice. He said that she knew Piggott. Then I went to her house, and Piggott was there a couple of times. He doesn't look like a criminal, but he laughs too much. It makes you distrustful."

"Why was Fleming there last night?" He glanced at his watch, and anxiety crawled in him.

"I told him I loved her. That we were almost engaged. Fleming wouldn't believe me. I told him to wait outside, last night, I could prove it easily. He thought that if I were right, she could help us.

"I walked down to his car. This was after the accident. There was lightning on the horizon, like a bad movie. I told him they'd been recording everything I said. He laughed and said he knew it. I asked to see his gun. I didn't tell him about Sue. When I shot, there was all this light. I thought lightning had struck by us. Then it smelled like blood and toilets. I wiped off the gun. I wrote it all down. You just have to read it."

Ralston asked gently, "I don't understand. Why did you shoot Fleming?"

"He would have known right off I killed her. He said she was working for Piggott."

His head shook blindly, and he jerked forward in his seat.

"He would have been sorry for me. I couldn't have faced him if he had known. Isn't that a dumb reason? It doesn't even make sense. But she told me she wouldn't have given the cassettes to Piggott. She told me. She loved me. We were almost engaged.

"You and I," he said, "would have been brothers-in-law."

169

He lifted his head.

"Are you corrupt, Mr. Ralston?"

"Not always," Ed said at last. He glanced again at his watch, and his heart pulsed. "Will you come with me and make a formal statement?"

"I wrote it down."

"We still need a statement."

"OK."

He rose slowly, a sleepwalker awake in his dream. He looked slowly around the room. "This is real, isn't it? I keep thinking that I'm going to wake up, but I am awake."

Ralston said, "You better hurry. I think Piggott knows you were there last night. He knows Sue . . . had an accident. He'll want to ask you about it."

"I pushed her away from me and she fell."

"He doesn't know that."

"It's just that simple. I pushed her away and she fell."

"We have got to get moving."

He followed the boy into the bedroom, watched him find a coat, pick up wallet, keys, money from the dresser.

"Not that." He took a fat pocketknife from Tommy's fingers.

"Dad gave me that."

"You'll get it back. Better give me the cassettes, too."

"Sure."

They left the apartment. Driving rain lashed their faces. As they came into the parking lot, a black sedan

170

jerked to a stop before them. Its doors opened, like an insect spreading its wings, and Buddy and Elmer bobbed out.

Ralston whispered urgently, "You left the house early. Nothing happened."

"But that's a lie," Tommy said.

The two men splashed toward them. Buddy's mouth was opened. He stopped before Ralston, hunching in the rain, hands jammed into his pockets. "Goin' somewhere, Champ?"

Elmer said, "Hello, Tommy. I think we met once at Sue's. Mr. Piggott would appreciate it if you could stop by and see him."

Tommy nodded gravely. "I'd like to see him. I have a lot to say."

Elmer looked respectfully at Ralston. "Mind if we borrow him, Ed?"

Ralston looked at Buddy's weighted pocket. He said, "I was just going that way, myself. Might as well join you."

They sat in the rear seat of the rain-whipped car. Elmer drove. Buddy, in the front seat, sat turned, looking at them.

Tommy lay back on the brown leather upholstery, his unshaven face wan in the pale light. His eyes were closed. His lips twitched and jerked with internal dialogue.

When they had driven for a quarter of an hour, he said unexpectedly, "Mr. Ralston?"

"Yes?"

"It feels—it's rather complicated to describe. It's as if I had been walking along someplace high and it fell apart under my feet. I feel as if I am in the act of falling. I'm suspended. I haven't started to fall yet. But I will. I don't understand how I feel. Is that guilt?"

"It's lack of sleep."

"I think it is the perception of guilt."

"Get some sleep if you can. Keep quiet and get some sleep."

Buddy said sharply, "Nobody asked you, Ralston. Let the kid talk. What'd you do, kid?"

Tommy's unkempt head threshed right and left.

Ralston jerked hands from pockets as he said, "Tommy, keep quiet," in a savage voice.

"Can it, Ralston," Buddy said.

"Screw you."

Buddy's arm flashed across the seat. He hit Ralston on the side of the head with a revolver. Ralston grunted and, trying to turn, was struck twice more.

He let himself fall loosely into Tommy's lap. To his surprise, he felt himself rising very swiftly up a shimmering incline. As he rose, he thrust the knife he had taken from his pocket into Tommy's hand. Light turned about him in an expanding spiral, and his speed became infinite.

He awoke almost at once. His nose and cheek were pressed against Tommy's coat. Elmer was snarling at Buddy with soft violence. Tommy was saying, "Mr. Ralston, Mr. Ralston," his voice horrified. The blows,

Ralston decided, had not been hard. He reasoned methodically that the angle for striking was wrong, and therefore insufficient leverage existed for a forceful blow. This conclusion amused him. Tommy's coat faded away.

When it returned, he heard Tommy saying: "You're bleeding."

"Let it bleed," he muttered.

He levered himself erect. His stomach pitched with the movement of the automobile and, when he moved his head, pain flared, stabbed hot channels down his neck. He closed his eyes and laid his head back against the seat and bled on Piggott's upholstery until the car stopped. He felt triumphant, in an obscure way.

The door opened. Ralston worked his legs from the car, gingerly hauled himself out. Rain flew against his face. Pain hammered his skull, and nausea still worked in him. He stood swaying, both hands clamped on the car door until his footing steadied.

Buddy stood smirking by the open door.

Ralston hit him on the side of the jaw. The effort threw white fire through his head. He fell to his knees. Buddy tumbled back against the side of the car, striking his head on the fender. He lay in the rain, eyes blinking.

Ralston staggered up, got his hand in Buddy's pocket, removed a heavy .38 with a walnut handle, a beautiful weapon. He stood swaying as Elmer glided around the side of the car.

Looking down at Buddy, Elmer said, "He never got past the third round, anytime."

"Let him lay," Ralston said, with effort.

"Gotta take him in," Elmer said. He and Tommy hoisted Buddy between them, hauled him loose-legged, foul-mouthed, into the white hall. They flopped him into a chair, walked toward Piggott's office. The ham-faced youngster bumbled up from his chair, stared round-eyed at them.

"Mr. Piggott's busy," he said.

"Go back to sleep," Ralston said, and pushed the door open.

Piggott was working at his table, shuffling papers with two other men. He looked sharply up as Ralston came in, then began to chuckle. "Ed, it must have been a strenuous morning." He glanced at the two men. "Boys, let's chase this around again in half an hour, OK?"

They left silently, not looking around, their arms full of paper.

Tommy, at the table now, looking down on Piggott, asked, "Mr. Piggott, why did you feel it necessary to involve Sue?" His voice was formal and mildly curious. "I mean—I should say, in your efforts to entrap me."

Glee illuminated Piggott's face. "Lordy, Tommy, there wasn't a thing personal. You're a real nice boy. Sue just completely enjoyed it."

Amusement shook his shoulders. He added, "Now, don't you take it too hard. Women just fool men all the time. It's their way."

Tommy said in a clipped voice, shoving hands into

his pockets, "I blamed her at first. I made a serious mistake. I should have realized that you were responsible. I was most certainly warned. But she would never have turned those cassettes over to you. She loved me, and she wouldn't have countenanced blackmail."

Incredulous delight lifted Piggott's shoulders. "Tommy, my friend, you are one of a kind. You really are."

"She loved me. We were going to get engaged."

Piggott's laughter poured into Tommy's face, a stream of sound. "Son, she did a real job on you. Not that she didn't like you. She thought you were grand. You just look here."

He tossed the engagement photograph across the table.

He said, "I was marrying her next month, Tommy. You were just a mite late."

"I love her," Tommy said, looking at the photograph. His voice began breaking up. "You never did."

The hall door came open hard, and Buddy came into the room, taking neat little steps. In his plaster face the eyes were terrible things. He called, "You, Ralston." A silver pistol jetted from his clasped hands.

Laughter stiffened on Piggott's face. In an unfamiliar voice, the texture of metal, he said, "Buddy, did I call . . ."

"I love her," Tommy said again.

He executed a fencer's flowing movement, an arc of graceful force that glided up the leg to the curved body to the extended right arm. His knife blade glinted as it entered Piggott's throat. His shoulders heaved with effort as he slashed right.

Incoherent noise tore from Piggott and a sudden scarlet jetting. He fell back in his chair, his expression amazed. His feet beat the floor. The chair toppled over with a heavy noise.

Gunfire, sudden, violent, repetitious, battered the room.

Tommy was slammed face forward onto the table. Papers cascaded, and a single yellow pencil spun across the pecan carpet.

The gunfire continued.

Pieces jumped out of the tabletop as Tommy's legs collapsed. He sprawled across the table, right arm extended, body jerking.

Buddy darted forward, the revolver bright in his brown hand, concentration wrinkling his face. He fired into Tommy's back.

Ralston shot him in the side of the head. Buddy fell over sideways and his gun, bounding across the floor, thudded against a gray filing cabinet.

Ralston whirled, knelt, looked down his gunsights into the enormous hollow hole of the .45 in Elmer's hand.

Confused shouting in the hallway.

Elmer said, white-lipped, "There's not five-cents profit for more shooting, Ed."

"No."

"We'd best put the guns up."

"All right."

The thumping of feet behind the table had stopped.

Men poured into the room.

Ralston sucked air, roared, "I'm Ed Ralston of the Sheriff's Department. This is police business, and I want this room cleared." He paced savagely toward them, face rigid, eyes gleaming, the horror in him intolerably bright.

Their faces glared anger, fear, shock. His voice beat at them. Elmer pushed at them, a confusion of voices and shoving bodies.

After one lifetime or two, the room emptied. Ralston shoved the gun away, said, "I'll call the sheriff."

"You might want to give us maybe half an hour. Some of the boys might want to fade. Give them a chance to get packed."

"Fifteen minutes. It'll have to be fifteen minutes."

Elmer nodded. "See you around, Ed."

The door closed and he was alone with the dead.

The strength leaked out of his body. He dropped into a chair and began to shake. His head blazed with pain. He could not control the shaking, which continued on and on.

Outside, engines began to roar, and he heard automobiles begin to go.

At last he wavered up on fragile legs, took a tissue from his pocket, and approached the table. Splinter-rimmed holes pocked the wood. He removed Tommy's wallet, took thirty of the sixty-two dollars. When he replaced the wallet, the body shifted and he thought that it would slip from the table to press its torn back against him. He wrenched back, white-faced. The body did not move again.

Piggott's wallet contained nearly six thousand dollars. Ralston removed four thousand in fifties and hundreds, counting them out slowly. He returned the wallet to a pocket the blood had not touched.

"They can both help bury her," he said.

His voice sounded stiff and high.

"We're all dead together," he said. He began to laugh.

When he heard himself, he became suddenly silent. Hard rain whipped the windows.

At last, his hand reached for the telephone.

Family Butcher

GEORGE SIMS

*George Sims's suspense stories are marked by his
ability to create an atmosphere in which unusual
action is made convincing, as in the postcard-
village setting of "Family Butcher." The author
of eleven books, Mr. Sims is a rare-book dealer in
Berkshire, England.*

PASTERNE is arguably the prettiest village in
the Hambleden Valley. Skirmett, Frieth,
Fingest, and Ibstone all have their attractions as does
Hambleden itself, and Turville is surmounted by a
delightful windmill perched on a hilltop, a rarity indeed in the Chilterns, but Pasterne most conforms to
a picture-postcard village. There is the large green,
immaculately trimmed, known as Pasterne Pound,

with carefully preserved oak stocks, and a dozen brick-and-flint cottages grouped round the green, just as if some Edwardian watercolourist had placed them there for a painting. The village pond is a fine example too, kept fresh by a spring, with white ducks and mallards and occasionally a nesting pair of swans. Postcards on sale in the village stores-cum-post office sell well in the summer months, particularly those featuring the pond and the rather eccentrically placed Norman church, which appears to have turned its back on Pasterne due to its being the sole relic of an even earlier settlement. But people in picture-postcard villages live lives much the same as the rest of us.

Another popular view of the village shows a northern aspect of the Pound with Daniel Patchin's butcher shop centrally placed, together with his Pound Cottage and the copse which hides Lord Benningworth's manor house. Patchin's shop was originally an Elizabethan cottage; it has been a good deal refurbished over the centuries, but the exterior, apart from the small shop window, must appear much as it did originally with its massive black oak beams and the plaster walls that are freshly whitewashed each year. The name *Daniel Patchin* is in large white italic letters on the black facade, together with the trade description FAMILY BUTCHER in smaller capitals.

Patchin's ancient establishment and the post office stores are the only village shops. Both are attractive and "quaint," looking rather like the toy shops favoured by children of less-sophisticated epochs. And Patchin's shop too is a model one, for he is fanatical about personal cleanliness and hygiene: he wears a fresh apron twice a day, and the washbasin at the rear of the shop is much used but kept spotless, as are the display area and the large bench where Patchin works, "looking more like a surgeon than a butcher," as Lord Benningworth once described him to some friends. Patchin's shop window always has a sparse display: a brace of pheasants, which he may well have shot himself, a hare, a local chicken or two, and one specimen of the prime meat he has for sale. Inside the shop there is a similarly small amount of meat on show: very likely just a side of Scotch beef hanging up with a Welsh shoulder of lamb. Under the impeccable refrigerated display counter there will be some of the famous Patchin sausages. Anything else that is required Daniel Patchin will have to fetch from the large cold room which takes up most of the rear portion of the shop.

The same shop when run by Daniel's father Gabriel was well known throughout the Chilterns in the 1930s, as was Reuben Patchin's before that. Daniel Patchin has an equally enviable reputation. Though the population of the village is not large enough to support such a thriving business, and Lord Benningworth who owns most of the village and the surrounding land is against more houses being built locally, callers come regularly from High Wycombe, Henley, and Marlow for their meat. The Patchin sausages are still made exactly as detailed in Reuben's 1912 recipe, with generous amounts of pork, herbs, spices and freshly ground black pepper; they bear no resemblance at all to the products churned out in factories, and they attract customers from as far away as Slough and Oxford.

Daniel Patchin, a quiet, sometimes taciturn, man, is widely respected. He seems to live for his work and is busy throughout a long day for five-and-a-half days each week. Wednesday is early closing, and that afternoon he devotes either to fishing or shooting according to the season. When he returned from the Korean war, Daniel Patchin came to an amicable unwritten agreement with Lord Benningworth that on Sundays he would act as an unpaid forester for the estate, keeping Benningworth's copses and woodland in good order, felling all diseased trees and clearing undergrowth, in return for which service he was allowed to keep all the timber he wanted. Every Sunday is devoted to this occupation, and Patchin has a woodyard at the back of his cottage where villagers can purchase logs and firewood.

The Patchin family has lived in Pasterne for centuries, but the Benningworth connection with the locality is even more ancient: Lord Benningworth can trace his ancestry back in this country to a Baron Will de Benningworth in 1220, and there are stone effigies of another Benningworth knight and his Lady installed in the church in 1290. The churchyard also houses many Patchin graves, but the earliest is dated 1695 with the epitaph:

Good people all as you
Pas by looke round
See how Corpes' do lye

For as you are some time Ware We
and as we are so must you be

Occasionally in an evening Daniel Patchin may
stroll round the churchyard eyeing the graves, particularly those of his own family. He likes those epitaphs
which hint of un-Christian attitudes, for he has a
cynical, mordant sense of humour; he is not a church-
goer. During his army service in Korea he found out
that human life there was as cheap as that of turkeys
at Christmas, and he adopted a stoic's attitude to life
and death. Serving as an infantryman he was awarded
the Military Medal for his bravery in hand-to-hand
fighting and won the nickname "pig-sticker" from his
comrades for his skill with the bayonet.

Daniel Patchin leads a very quiet life, devoted to
work and country pursuits, including gardening in the
evenings. Lord Benningworth will sometimes stroll to
the edge of his copse with a friend to point out
Patchin's garden with its fine rose beds and lines of
potatoes, peas, and beans as straight as guardsmen on
parade. Patchin's wife Angela is ten years younger
than him and before the marriage was known as a
pretty, jolly, and slightly flighty girl in Skirmett, where
she was brought up in a large farming family. The
Patchins have no children, as Angela proved to be
barren, and over the ten years of marriage she has
taken on the Patchin family's traits of seriousness and
quiet outward mildness. She is a natural blonde with
very fair, clear skin who blushes easily: any compli-
ment from Benningworth's son and heir before he

left to work in America would always make her change colour. She works behind the till in a cubiclelike office in the shop on Patchin's busiest days, always on Friday and Saturday, and occasionally on Thursday. Patchin employs a boy who makes himself generally useful on Friday evenings and Saturday mornings; otherwise he does all the work himself. He is a stocky man with massive muscles, enormously strong. Behind the shop there is a large shed which was used for all the slaughtering for the business up till about twenty years ago, and that is where Patchin dispatches local poultry and scores of turkeys and geese at Christmas.

It was on a glorious late May afternoon that Daniel Patchin first became suspicious of his wife. It was a Monday, and at lunch she had said that she would go for a walk in the afternoon. Returning at five, she looked in at the shop to ask if he would like a cup of tea. He nodded and asked if she had enjoyed the walk. She hesitated, and he looked up from the mincing machine to see that she had blushed and was nervously fiddling with the buttons on her blouse as if to make sure they were all fastened. It would be difficult to imagine a more observant man than Daniel Patchin: his whole life both at work and during his time away from the shop had sharpened his perceptions. He had made a lifetime study of his customers and of nature; it was his sole inactive hobby. The slightest change in a pensioner's expression, even the movement of an eye, was enough to tell Patchin that he was proffering a too-expensive piece of meat; the faintest ripple at the end of a roach "swim" caught his notice, as did the sound of a twig snapping. When she did not reply about the obvious pleasures of a country walk on a perfect May afternoon, Patchin covered his wife's loss for words with a quick comment about an old woman who always called in for broth bones on a Monday.

When Angela left the shop, Patchin gave her back an intense look, noting that she had changed completely from the clothes she had worn at lunch. When she returned with the tray of tea, she had covered her pretty white blouse with an old brown cardigan. She was still nervous, restless, very slightly ill at ease. Patchin knew that she was a hopeless liar but did not ask any more questions. There was a fresh smell of lemon soap, and Patchin knew she had washed her face, probably plunging it repeatedly into cold water to get rid of the faint, pink flush. Again he covered her silence with talk of how he might go down to the river that evening. The season for coarse fishing did not start till mid-June, but it was something he occasionally did out of season, inspecting favourite angling haunts to see how they had been affected by the high level of the Thames in winter.

During the next few weeks he added to his short list of pastimes the one of observing his wife: nothing that she did escaped him, even the merest hint of exasperation or frustration was filed away silently in his head—but nothing unusual ever attracted a comment from him.

It would not have required special ability as an observer to note Angela Patchin's revived interest in her clothes; even on Monday mornings when she did her weekly wash and on Wednesdays when she usually cleaned Pound Cottage from top to bottom she stopped wearing her old navy skirt and blossomed out in a new green one worn with a pretty apron or jeans. She went to the Marks and Spencer store in Reading ostensibly to buy a summer frock but returned with several packages.

One Monday afternoon when Angela had gone for another walk, Patchin closed the shop for a quarter of an hour and thoroughly inspected her chest of drawers. He took meticulous care in moving and replacing the various things; he found several new items of underwear, including a particularly skimpy pair of knickers and a brassiere designed to thrust size thirty-six breasts up and outwards as if proffering them to some lusty lad in a Restoration play. But which lusty lad? That was the question that teased Daniel Patchin's brain, taking his attention away from his work so that he tended for the first time in his life to become a little absentminded and not quite the usual model of efficiency. It was immediately noted by the villagers—"Seems more human somehow" was the general verdict, though expressed in different ways.

For a while Patchin speculated as to whether Lord Benningworth's son had returned to Pasterne and was again flattering Angela. If so, it seemed a more serious matter than before, now apparently extending to her amply filled blouse. But an inquiry, casually phrased, to the Benningworth's housekeeper informed Patchin that the heir to the estate was still working happily in

New York and did not plan to return home before Christmas.

Patchin's reaction to Angela's unusual behaviour varied considerably. At times he became quite fascinated by his secret observation in a detached way, as he had once studied an elusive old pike in a pool near Hambleden Mill: for weeks throughout one autumn he had tried various baits to entice the wily monster until he realised that the pike could be stirred into action only by a fish with fresh blood on it; so Patchin had served up a dace, liberally doused in blood, and the pike had succumbed. At other times Patchin experienced a feeling of cold fury that someone was stealing his wife from him; he was quite certain that it was happening. Once he woke with a horrid start in the middle of the night, convinced that the telephone had rung just once, and then lay awake consumed with feelings of jealousy and twisted lust; he did not fall asleep till just before the alarm bell rang at six.

Perhaps Angela's changed attitude to sex was the most obvious giveaway. Before the Monday afternoon walks and the new clothes, she seemed to have regarded it as a rather boring routine matter to be managed as quickly as possible before turning away to sleep. Now she never turned away and was always ready for sex, keener than he could ever remember her being. Her kisses were open-mouthed and lingering, her embraces passionate and urgent; as he brooded on this he realised that "urgent" was the key word—that

187

was it, she was urging him on to more effort so that he resembled, when her eyes were closed, her other, very passionate lover. Even after an orgasm she was unsatisfied, longing for something else. It would be impossible to describe the various feelings Patchin experienced as his wife became ever more knowing in bed, with wanton behaviour and explicit movements trying to get him to obtain the results she enjoyed elsewhere. One night she wanted him to make love in a new position, and as she determinedly pushed him into place he could see the grim joke of it so clearly that he nearly laughed. Nothing could make it more plain that Angela had a very virile, enthusiastic lover, much more skilled at the amatory arts than he would ever be, a lover who liked first to be inflamed by skimpy knickers and a "display" brassiere and then performed perfectly.

It was not until a Friday in the middle of June that Patchin was able to identify his enemy. He disturbed Angela while she was making a phone call when he entered Pound Cottage that lunch time a few minutes earlier than usual. As he opened the door, the telephone was slammed down, and Angela ran upstairs to cover her confusion. That afternoon Ray Johnson, the youngest postman in the area, called in at the shop ostensibly for a pound of sausages and some bacon. Johnson grinned over at Angela in the little office, calling out, "Afternoon, Mrs. Patchin." Angela did not reply but just nodded, flushing very slightly. Apart from that telltale flush there was something subtle about the way Johnson addressed her, with just an inflection of the "Mrs. Patchin," as though the formal mode of address was something of a joke between the pair. Daniel Patchin took his time in the cold storage room to give them a chance for a few words. The moment he opened the door, Ray Johnson stopped talking and grinned foolishly as though he had forgotten what he was going to say.

Idiot, Patchin thought, you young idiot, but passed over the momentary awkwardness for Johnson by commenting on the sausages: "Cook's specials this lot. Part of a batch I made up for the Manor. The old man likes just an extra pinch of pepper."

Having once seen his wife with Johnson, there was no longer any doubt in Patchin's mind, for it seemed to him as if there were some invisible but subtly tangible connection between them, an unspoken intimacy born of their long afternoons together, probably in Calcot Wood where there were some idyllic glades. As he did up the bacon and sausages and the embarrassed couple said nothing, Patchin could visualise them on a greensward in a patch of dappled sunlight, the flimsy knickers being removed together with the trick brassiere, and then Angela's urgent movements as the mutual madness began. Patchin felt as though his obsessive thoughts might show on his usually phlegmatic face, so he cleared his throat loudly and shook his head, saying, "Sorry. Throat's a bit sore. Hope it's not a summer cold."

Ray Johnson gave Patchin an unusually serious, not altogether friendly look as he replied, "Yes. Let's hope not." The look negated the banal response, and Patchin

thought, Liar; it would please you if I came down
with pneumonia. For the first time it struck him that
the feeling of jealousy might not all be on one side.
Probably Johnson was also jealous of the nights when
Patchin slept with Angela; possibly Johnson was coming to hate him as he had hated the unknown lover.

Later that afternoon, when Angela had gone back
to the cottage to make some tea, Daniel Patchin stood
at the open door of the shop staring at the pond where
a pair of Canada geese had alighted and were being
harried and made unwelcome by the aggressive, though
small, coots which dashed in and out of the reeds,
making proprietorial noises. And indeed Patchin did
not miss anything that happened on the pond, noting
how the mallards vanished and the white ducks kept
out of the noisy quarrel like only faintly interested
spectators. But Patchin's mind was elsewhere, brood-
ing on his predicament: it was the first time since the
Korean war that Patchin felt he was faced with a problem he did not know how to handle. Ray Johnson was
a tall, slight lad with curly black hair and a mouth
that always seemed to be open, either grinning or
laughing to show very white teeth. Johnson was easily
the most popular of the local postmen; he was extremely cheerful, full of banter and old jokes. Patchin
had always found that slightly irritating—but now
the trifling feeling of irritation was replaced by the
strong one of implacable enmity. Patchin had no intention of confronting Angela with his suspicions or
of trying to surprise the lovers in the act, even though
he thought it could be arranged one Monday after-

noon in Calcot Wood. For all he knew, Angela might then decide to leave him—he did not know how heavily their reasonably prosperous and comfortable life together weighed against the hours of passion spent with Lothario Johnson. No, the only answer was to get rid of him as the coots would undoubtedly rid themselves of the intruding Canada geese.

After the break for tea, Patchin got down to work again. Friday evening was one of his busiest times, as dozens of joints had to be prepared for the weekend— he had some particularly choosy customers who liked to have their meat prepared in the finicky French manner, and he was quite willing to cater to their tastes. A great deal of beef had been ordered for that weekend, and his young assistant was not up to preparing it, being capable of carrying out only the humblest jobs. Patchin set the boy to mincing pork and then began butchering two sides of beef, attacking the carcase with relish.

Once supper was finished, he could hardly wait to get Angela to bed: knowing that she was the young man's mistress had the strange, unexpected effect of doubling his lust for her. And she seemed equally ready for sex, falling back on the bed and raising her knees, smiling at him in a new way, a smile that contained a hint of amusement at his fumbling efforts to please her. This time it was his turn to be left feeling unsatisfied and empty even though he took her twice, as if possessing her half-a-dozen times would not be enough to assuage his restless yearning.

From mid-June, Daniel Patchin spent most of his

Sundays in Calcot Wood; it was by far the largest area of woodland owned by Lord Benningworth. One Sunday he decided to devote to searching for clues as to the lovers' meetingplace and did come on a bed of crushed ferns; it left him with a strange sensation and feeling slightly sick. From the improvised bed he made his way down to a deserted cottage in the remotest part of the wood, a spot that never seemed to be reached by the sun, as it stood in the shadow of Calcot Hill. It had been a gamekeeper's cottage up to 1939, but the prewar Benningworth regime of having a gamekeeper had been dropped, and the remote, unattractive cottage was let, when Patchin was a youth, to a strange old man called Ted Ames, then left to rot. Lord Benningworth was a true conservative in that he was against change of any kind, even that of having a wreck of a building knocked down. The old widower Ames had eventually gone off his head and been taken away to a mental hospital in 1948, where he died. Since then the cottage had been stripped of its gutters and drainpipes; most of the roof was still sound, but rain had dripped in through a few missing tiles and some of the rafters were rotten, covered in mould; even on the warmest summer day the old cottage smelt of dank decay. There was fungus on the kitchen walls, and weeds were gradually invading the ground-floor rooms, sprouting up from the cracks in the brick floors.

Daniel Patchin stood absolutely still for a long while, staring at the ruined building which some villagers claimed was haunted by Ted Ames. Patchin did not believe in ghosts, spirits, heaven or hell: he believed that the universe was incomprehensible and absolutely indifferent to mankind. Suddenly he said aloud, "What a waste. Pity not to make some use of the old place." The second sentence, spoken in a particularly mild voice, ended on a faintly questioning note, and for the first time he moved his head as though he were talking to someone and waiting for a comment on his suggestion. Then he gave the idea, engendered by his memory of a certain feature of the ancient fireplace in Ames's kitchen, a mirthless smile and turned on his heel.

Throughout Calcot Wood there were piles of logs that Patchin built till he was ready to remove a truckload. There was also a hut where he kept a chain saw, tins of petrol, axes, and bags of wood chips and sawdust. He looked around to make sure that there was no one about and began to carry sacks of sawdust and chippings over to the cottage; he felt great satisfaction in commencing work on his plan.

On succeeding Sundays Daniel Patchin spent a good deal of time in transporting dry branches and brushwood; he also used his van to move cans of paraffin, half-empty tins of paint, plastic bags that had contained dripping, sacks of fat, soiled rags, and other rubbish. These he carefully planted throughout the cottage, gradually turning it into a massive potential bonfire.

While the preparations in Calcot Wood were proceeding satisfactorily, Patchin made a study of Ray Johnson's working life. By casual questions to the village postmistress, who delighted in gossip, he wormed out the routine of Johnson and other postmen in the area. One of his discoveries was that Johnson often had either Monday or Wednesday afternoon off, and this was confirmed for him on the first Wednesday in July when Angela took a surprising interest in his fishing plans for that afternoon. Usually she was bored by angling, so he answered these questions with concealed, wry humour. Then, prompted by a whim, he took more time than usual in his preparations for the weekly expedition to the Thames. His fishing equipment was the simplest that could be devised—he despised the "London crowd" who invaded the river at weekends weighed down with paraphernalia. He had an all-purpose rod, a few hooks and floats, and one reel carried in an army haversack. As he pretended to fuss over these things and to take an unusually long time in making the flour paste for bait, he could see that Angela was very much on edge, nervous, and yet pleasurably excited at the same time. She had not mentioned going out, so he suspected that there might be a plan for Johnson to visit Pound Cottage while he was away. While the cat's away the mice will play, he said over and over in his mind as he rolled the ball of dough between his strong, dry fingers.

When he at last set off in the van, he was again ironically amused that Angela came out to wave goodbye, as though to be certain of his departure. Patchin spent an hour on the riverbank but was not in the mood for fishing. The reeds were haunted by colourful dragonflies, and there was a brief darting visit from a kingfisher—sights that usually pleased him, but on this occasion he was hardly aware of anything about him, feeling rather like a ghost returned to haunt the scene of past pleasures.

Patchin drove back from the Thames with not much heart for what lay immediately ahead, but he now felt it was essential to make quite sure of the situation. In Pasterne he parked his van by the pond and appeared to stare down into its clear water for a while. Such behaviour on his part would not excite comment, for he had been known to catch sticklebacks and frogs there to use as bait when angling for pike.

After some minutes of staring with unseeing eyes, Patchin ambled back to his closed shop then walked through it into the garden that led up to Pound Cottage. He trod noiselessly over the lawn and entered the side door very quietly. Within a minute his suspicions were dramatically confirmed: through the board ceiling that separated the living room from the bedroom he heard the squeaking springs of his double bed, squeaking so loudly that it seemed as if the springs were protesting at the extraordinary behaviour of the adulterous couple. Then there began a peculiar rhythmic grunting noise, and his wife called out something incomprehensible in a strange voice.

Patchin retreated noiselessly, got back into his car, and returned to Hambleden Mill. He fished stolidly for three hours with a dour expression on his face, an expression that some North Korean soldiers had probably glimpsed before he killed them with his bayonet. Usually he returned small fish to the river, but on that afternoon he just ripped them off the hook and threw them on the bank.

Returning home again at about his usual time, Patchin found his wife in an excellent mood. Fornication seemed to be good for her health, as she appeared blooming. A delicious supper had been prepared for him, and Angela had popped over to the village stores to buy a bottle of the dry cider he favoured. She looked quite fetching with her flushed cheeks, her curly blonde hair freshly washed, and the two top buttons of a new pink blouse left undone, but Patchin could not respond at all; momentarily he found it difficult to keep up the pretence of not knowing about her affair and felt as though an expression of suspicion and cold contempt must appear on his face. When he went to wash he stared in the mirror and was surprised to find the usual phlegmatic expression reflected.

After supper Angela wanted to stroll around in the garden. It was something Patchin normally enjoyed, seeing the results of all his hard work, for in June the garden looked at its best, with the rose beds "a picture," as Angela said, and usually it was very satisfactory to inspect the neat rows of vegetables. Instead he experienced a most unusual mood of emptiness and frustration: everything seemed hollow and meaningless.

While his wife bent down to smell a rose, Daniel Patchin stared up at the clear evening sky. He knew his enjoyment of life was temporarily lost and that it would not return until he was rid of the man who threatened his marriage. Angela came and stood by him, took his hand, and placed it on her firm, round breast, an action that would have been quite out of character a few months before; but her new sensuality did not move him at all, and when they went to bed, making love to her was like a ritual, quite spoilt by his memory of the protesting bedsprings.

Patchin decided to try to put his plan of murder into effect on the second Wednesday in July. Angela went for a walk again on the Monday of that week, so according to his understanding of the postman's routine, it seemed probable that Ray Johnson would be working on the Wednesday afternoon. If so, he would then be driving down the narrow lane that skirted Calcot Wood to clear a remote, little-used postbox about 3 P.M.

On the Wednesday, Patchin felt quite calm and confident that everything would go as he devised. He set off from Pound Cottage promptly at 2 P.M. after an excellent lunch of roast loin of pork with the first new potatoes from the garden and a large helping of broad beans. His haversack had been got ready on the previous evening. It now contained some other things as well as fishing tackle: rubber gloves, matches, a ball of extremely tough cord, sticking plasters, and a foot-long piece of iron pipe.

Parking his van just off the lane by the wood in a cunningly chosen spot where it would not be seen, Patchin took his haversack and walked quickly through the wood to Ames's cottage. He experienced pleasurable excitement in doing so and in inspecting the fire he had laid in the kitchen grate. It consisted of three fire lighters, paper spills and wood chippings, a few sticks, and numerous small pieces of coal. It had been constructed with the care that a chaffinch gives to making its nest, and he estimated that it would burn intensely for an hour or two. "Quite long enough to roast a joint," he said in an expressionless voice as he got up from his crouching position in front of the grate.

After inspecting the trails of wood chippings soaked in paraffin which he had laid throughout the cottage like long fuses leading to explosive charges, he glanced round the wildly overgrown plot that had once been a garden. Rank grass a foot high contended with massive clumps of nettles, giant docks, and cow parsley. He did not think that it would be possible to trace footprints on such a terrain, but also he did not expect his enterprise to be risk-free. There were bound to be risks in a life governed by mere chance.

It was 2:45 P.M. when he walked back through the wood to the narrow, twisting lane. He wore the rubber gloves; his left hand was in his old fishing-jacket pocket and the other was plunged into the haversack that hung from his right shoulder. He positioned himself in the lane so that he would be on the driver's side of the van when it approached him. The oppressive mood which had dogged him for so many weeks had lifted, and he whistled as he waited—a rather tuneless version of "As Time Goes By," which he repeated over and over again.

At 3 P.M. precisely he heard a motor engine in the lane and got ready to wave the van down if it was driven by Johnson. For the first time that afternoon excitement seized him, with a thumping of his heart and a sudden tremor of fear such as he had always experienced before hand-to-hand fighting in Korea. He had once said to another soldier there, "Everyone's afraid at times. Anyone who says he isn't is either a liar or a fool."

As the post office van came round the corner, Patchin waved it down, first tentatively then more vigorously as he spotted Johnson's head of black curly hair. Johnson stopped the van, rolled its window farther down, and called out, "What's up?"

Patchin walked slowly across to the van, limping very slightly and holding himself as though he were in pain. "Sorry, sorry," he said. "Bit of trouble." He came close to the van door and stood silent, with his eyes half-closed and swaying slightly as though he were going to faint.

With a puzzled expression in which there was just the faintest hint of suspicion, Johnson opened the van door and began to get out—his height made doing so a rather awkward business. Patchin took out the iron pipe and hit Johnson on the head, a measured blow by someone who had considerable experience in stunning animals. Johnson lurched forward and then fell in a heap, just like a poleaxed bullock. Patchin bundled him back into the van, got into the driving seat, and drove off down the lane, whistling the same tune again. After a hundred yards he turned off onto a track which led in the direction of the gamekeeper's cottage. Before leaving the red van he pressed Johnson's fingers on the steering wheel, then bundled the body up and carried it on his shoulder as easily as he managed a side of beef.

He also paused in the decaying doorway to impress Johnson's fingerprints on two empty paraffin cans, then carried him through to the kitchen. The tall man was still inert, but as Patchin dropped his burden onto the cement floor, Johnson's eyelids flickered. Patchin sat him up like a ventriloquist's dummy and then knocked him out with a blow to the jaw that would have floored most boxers.

Patchin put sticky plasters over Johnson's large mouth, then worked on the unconscious man with the skill he always showed in preparing joints. He put his legs neatly together and bound them tightly from above the knee to the ankles, using the same binding technique he used in repairing his fishing rod, pulling the cord so tight that the legs became immobile; he left a loop by the ankles. He repeated the process with the limp arms. Then came the part that gave him most satisfaction: lifting the two loops onto the hooks that had once supported a turnspit in front of the fire. Immediately after Johnson was suspended like an animal carcass ready to be roasted, Patchin lit the fire in the grate and left the cottage.

Before taking off his rubber gloves, Patchin picked up the empty paraffin cans and left them near the old garden gate, which was half hanging off its hinges, then strode off to the place where he had hidden his own van. The time was 3:30, and everything had gone exactly as he had hoped. There was always blind chance of course, for instance, the remote possibility that another pair of lovers might be trespassing in the woods and see him striding along so purposefully, but there was nothing he could do about it.

Driving to the Thames, Patchin mentally examined his plan again and formulated one or two more things to be done. As soon as he had parked the van near Hambleden Mill, he assembled his rod and line right down to putting on the bait, a thing he never did till he was actually on the riverbank, so that anyone seeing him might think he had already been fishing and was trying another spot. Then, carrying the assembled rod, he walked along a gravel path and over the complicated series of weirs which cross the Thames at Hambleden Mill. As he approached the lock, he watched to see whether the keeper there might be in sight and was relieved to be able to cross unseen.

Patchin threw his piece of iron pipe into the river before spending an hour angling. He fished like a young boy, close-in to the bank where there were more bites to be had but the fish were always small. He caught a tiny roach and three gudgeon but was quite satisfied with them, leaving the last gudgeon on the hook as he walked back to the lock. Good fortune was still with him, for the lockkeeper was now at work opening the gates for a motor cruiser. The keeper, who knew Patchin well, called out, "Any luck, Dan?"

"Not much. Just tiddlers," Patchin called out, shaking his rod so that the suspended gudgeon twisted about at the end of the line. "Think I'll use them to try for a pike in the pool by the mill. See you."

"Yes, see you. Will you keep me a nice small chicken for the weekend?"

"Yes. Right." Patchin walked off just fractionally quicker than he did normally. With excitement working in him at the prospect of revisiting Ames's cottage, it was not easy to appear just as usual. For once he was grateful that he had a rather expressionless face.

His mind on other things, he mechanically dismantled the fishing rod and line as quickly as he could. "Yes, all going to plan," he said aloud, though there was no one within a hundred yards of him.

Driving back to the lane once more he experienced a surprising feeling of letdown and anticlimax. It was true that it had all gone without a hitch as far as he could tell, but somehow it seemed a bit too easy. There would have been more satisfaction if he could have allowed the tall but puny Johnson a chance to fight, some ludicrous attempt at self-defence which he would have brushed away derisively, as easily as a tomcat deals with a rat.

Once in Calcot Wood again, Patchin's nose twitched. There was a faint aroma like that of roast pork which had greeted him at lunchtime at Pound Cottage. It grew stronger at every step he took. Desultory grey fumes struggled up from the ancient chimney. The smell was very strong in the hall and unpleasantly so in the kitchen, which reeked of cooking odours and where a blackened, twisted carcase was still roasting and dripping fat into a dying fire.

Despite the smell, Patchin stayed there looking at the object, which bore no resemblance to the once garrulous postman. Patchin's hatred of the man had quite disappeared now that there was no longer any need for it. He was not gloating over his victim but musing on the quintessential evanescence of man. How easily was man humbled, how soon was he changed into rotting meat! It had been just the same in Korea: one minute his friend Dusty Seddon had been telling a dirty joke, the next moment lying mute with most of his face blown off.

Pausing in the hall, Patchin set light to a pile of paraffin-soaked sawdust and then lit the trails of wood chips and retreated to the sagging front door, throwing the box of matches behind him.

The fire had taken a firm grip on the cottage before Patchin had even left the garden; he could hear it raging and roaring unseen until a sheet of flame sprang up at one of the diamond-leaded windows. For the second time that day, Patchin experienced a slight attack of nerves; momentarily his right hand shook, and for a few minutes he seemed to be walking on lifeless legs, having to make an extraordinary amount of effort just to propel himself along.

Seated in his van, Patchin took out a large handkerchief and wiped his forehead, which was sweating profusely, and allowed himself a few minutes' rest before driving off in his customary careful manner. Was there something he had overlooked, perhaps a trifling slip which might lead the police to his door in a few days' time? As he navigated a series of lanes and minor roads that would put him once again on the main road from Hambleden to Pasterne, his mind was exercised by the nagging suspicion that he might have made one vital mistake.

Calm gradually returned as he drove slowly along, and he began to think of the possible effect of the fire on the Benningworth estate. The large garden of rank grass and weeds should act as a barrier between the fire and Calcot Wood, but even if it did spread, Lord Benningworth owed him a favour for all the hard work he had put in there as amateur forester for twenty-five years. A sudden thought made Patchin smile. The Benningworth family motto, *Esse quam videre*, 'To be rather than to seem to be,' was well known in the locality; it was a pity that Ray Johnson had not known that Daniel Patchin also had a motto: "What I have I hold."

When Patchin arrived in Pasterne he felt completely normal. His pleasant life had been momentarily threatened with an upheaval, but that was now all over. The village looked particularly lovely in the late afternoon sunlight. The white ducks were sedulously paddling to and fro as though they were paid to do so, and swifts were skimming over the clear pond's mirrorlike surface, occasionally dipping down to it, hunting midges. The postmistress's black and white cat moved carefully over the neatly clipped grass as if it might be stalking a newt and sat down at the edge of the pond. "Pretty as a picture," Patchin said.

Walking along to Pound Cottage, Daniel Patchin thought of what he should say when he saw Angela. It was essential to appear absolutely as normal so that when she heard of the perplexing tragedy in Calcot

Wood nothing about his behaviour should prompt suspicion in her mind. Then he understood Angela's difficulty in appearing quite normal or saying anything about that walk she had taken on the glorious May afternoon, because phrases that he went over in his mind seemed artificial and suspicious. "Nice afternoon, but I didn't catch anything"—false. "I enjoyed it, but not good fishing weather"—unnatural.

But Patchin need not have worried, for as soon as he opened the side door he heard the squeak of protesting bedsprings and Angela calling out in a voice that sounded false and unnatural.

High Darktown

JAMES ELLROY

James Ellroy is a 38-year-old high school dropout who has displayed remarkable proficiency as a novelist. His first book, Brown's Requiem *was nominated for a Private Eye Writers of America* Shamus *Award. His second,* Clandestine, *was nominated for a Mystery Writers of America* Edgar *and won a medal from the* West Coast Review of Books. *His subsequent novels, from the Mysterious Press—*Blood on the Moon *and* Because the Night—*begin a quintet about LA policeman Lloyd Hopkins. The third volume,* Suicide Hill, *is scheduled for spring 1986.*

Lee Blanchard, the detective in "High Darktown," is a main character in Mr. Ellroy's novel-in-progress to be called The Black Dahlia. *The novel is based on a true crime case—the 1947 Los Angeles murder of a hauntingly beautiful black-clad woman. Mr. Ellroy hints that Blanchard will prove himself to be less than heroic.*

FROM MY OFFICE windows I watched L.A. celebrate the end of World War II. Central Division Warrants took up the entire north side of City Hall's eleventh floor, so my vantage point was high and wide. I saw clerks drinking straight from the bottle in the Hall of Records parking lot across the street and harness bulls forming a riot squad and heading for Little Tokyo a few blocks away, bent on holding back a conga line of youths with 2 by 4s who looked bent on going the atom bomb one better. Craning my neck, I glimpsed tall black plumes of smoke on Bunker Hill—a sure sign that patriotic Belmont High students were stripping cars and setting the tires on fire. Over on Sunset and Figueroa, knots of zooters were assembling in violation of the Zoot Suit Ordinance, no doubt figuring that today it was anything goes.

The tiny window above my desk had an eastern exposure, and it offered up nothing but smog and a giant traffic jam inching toward Boyle Heights. I stared into the brown haze, imagining shitloads of code 2s and 3s thwarted by noxious fumes and bumper-to-bumper revelry. My daydreams got more and more vivid, and when I had a whole skyful of A-bombs descending on the offices of the L.A.P.D. Detective Bureau, I slammed my desk and picked up the two pieces of paper I had been avoiding all morning.

The first sheet was a scrawled memo from the Daywatch Robbery boss down the hall: "Lee—Wallace Simpkins paroled from Quentin last week—to our jurisdiction. Thought you should know. Be careful. G.C."

Cheery V-J Day tidings.

The second page was an interdepartmental teletype issued from University Division, and, when combined with Georgie Caulkins's warning, it spelled out the beginning of a new one-front war.

Over the past five days there had been four heavy-muscle stickups in the West Adams district, perpetrated by a two-man heist team, one white, one negro. The MO was identical in all four cases: liquor stores catering to upper-crust negroes were hit at night, half an hour before closing, when the cash registers were full. A well-dressed male Caucasian would walk in and beat the clerk to the floor with the barrel of a .45 automatic, while the negro heister stuffed the till cash into a paper bag. Twice customers had been present when the robberies occurred; they had also been beaten senseless—one elderly woman was still in critical condition at Queen of Angels.

It was as simple and straightforward as a neon sign. I picked up the phone and called Al Van Patten's personal number at the County Parole Bureau.

"Speak, it's your nickel."

"Lee Blanchard, Al."

"Big Lee! You working today? The war's over!"

"No, it's not. Listen, I need the disposition on a parolee. Came out of Quentin last week. If he reported in, I need an address; if he hasn't, just tell me."

"Name? Charge?"

"Wallace Simpkins, 655 PC. I sent him up myself in '39."

Al whistled. "Light jolt. He got juice?"

"Probably kept his nose clean and worked a war industries job inside; his partner got released to the army after Pearl Harbor. Hurry it up, will you?"

"Off and running."

Al dropped the receiver to his desk, and I suffered through long minutes of static-filtered party noise—male and female giggles, bottles clinking together, happy county flunkies turning radio dials trying to find dance music but getting only jubilant accounts of the big news. Through Edward R. Murrow's uncharacteristically cheerful drone I pictured Wild Wally Simpkins, flush with cash and armed for bear, looking for *me*. I was shivering when Al came back on the line and said, "He's hot, Lee."

"Bench warrant issued?"

"Not yet."

"Then don't waste your time."

"What are you talking about?"

"Small potatoes. Call Lieutenant Holland at University dicks and tell him Simpkins is half of the heist team he's looking for. Tell him to put out an APB and add, 'armed and extremely dangerous' and 'apprehend with all force deemed necessary.' "

Al whistled again. "That bad?"

I said, "Yeah," and hung up. "Apprehend with all force deemed necessary" was the L.A.P.D. euphemism for "shoot on sight." I felt my fear decelerate just a notch. Finding fugitive felons was my job. Slipping an extra piece into my back waistband, I set out to find the man who had vowed to kill me.

After picking up standing mugs of Simpkins and a carbon of the robbery report from Georgie Caulkins, I drove toward the West Adams district. The day was hot and humid, and sidewalk mobs spilled into the street, passing victory bottles to horn-honking motorists. Traffic was bottlenecked at every stoplight, and paper debris floated down from office windows—a makeshift ticker-tape parade. The scene made me itchy, so I attached the roof light and hit my siren, weaving around stalled cars until downtown was a blur in my rearview mirror. When I slowed, I was all the way to Alvarado and the city I had sworn to protect looked normal again. Slowing to a crawl in the right-hand lane, I thought of Wallace Simpkins and knew the itch wouldn't stop until the bastard was bought and paid for.

We went back six years, to the fall of '39, when I was a vice officer in University Division and a regular light-heavyweight attraction at the Hollywood-Legion Stadium. A black–white stickup gang had been clouting markets and juke joints on West Adams, the white guy passing himself off as a member of Mickey Cohen's mob, coercing the proprietor into opening up the safe for the monthly protection payment while the negro guy looked around innocently, then hit the cash registers. When the white guy got to the safe, he took all the money, then pistol-whipped the proprietor senseless. The heisters would then drive slowly north into the respectable Wilshire district, the white guy at the wheel, the negro guy huddled down in the back seat.

I got involved in the investigation on a fluke.

After the fifth job, the gang stopped cold. A stoolie of mine told me that Mickey Cohen found out that the white muscle was an ex-enforcer of his and had him snuffed. Rumor had it that the colored guy—a cowboy known only as Wild Wallace—was looking for a new partner and a new territory. I passed the information along to the dicks and thought nothing more of it. Then, a week later, it all hit the fan.

As a reward for my tip, I got a choice moonlight assignment: bodyguarding a high-stakes poker game frequented by L.A.P.D. brass and navy bigwigs up from San Diego. The game was held in the back room at Minnie Roberts's Casbah, the swankiest police-sanctioned whorehouse on the south side. All I had to do was look big, mean, and servile and be willing to share boxing anecdotes. It was a major step toward sergeant's stripes and a transfer to the Detective Division.

It went well—all smiles and backslaps and recountings of my split-decision loss to Jimmy Bivins—until a negro guy in a chauffeur's outfit and an olive-skinned youth in a navy officer's uniform walked in the door. I saw a gun bulge under the chauffeur's left arm, and chandelier light fluttering over the navy man's face revealed pale negro skin and processed hair.

And I knew.

I walked up to Wallace Simpkins, my right hand extended. When he grasped it, I sent a knee into his balls and a hard left hook at his neck. When he hit the floor, I pinned him there with a foot on his gun bulge, drew my own piece, and leveled it at his partner. "Bon voyage, Admiral," I said.

The admiral was named William Boyle, an apprentice armed robber from a black bourgeois family fallen on hard times. He turned state's evidence on Wild Wallace, drew a reduced three-to-five jolt at Chino as part of the deal, and was paroled to the war effort early in '42. Simpkins was convicted of five counts of robbery one with aggravated assault, got five-to-life at Big Q, and voodoo-hexed Billy Boyle and me at his trial, vowing on the soul of Baron Samedi to kill both of us, chop us into stew meat, and feed it to his dog. I more than half believed his vow, and for the first few years he was away, every time I got an unexplainable ache or pain I thought of him in his cell, sticking pins into a blue-suited Lee Blanchard voodoo doll.

I checked the robbery report lying on the seat beside me. The addresses of the four new black–white stickups covered 26th and Gramercy to La Brea and Adams. Hitting the racial demarcation line, I watched the topography change from negligent middle-class white to proud colored. East of St. Andrews, the houses were unkempt, with peeling paint and ratty front lawns. On the west the homes took on an air of elegance: small dwellings were encircled by stone fencing and well-tended greenery; the mansions that had earned West Adams the sobriquet High Darktown put Beverly Hills pads to shame—they were older, larger, and less architecturally pretentious, as if the owners knew that the only way to be rich and black was to downplay the performance with the quiet noblesse oblige of old white money.

I knew High Darktown only from the scores of conflicting legends about it. When I worked University Division, it was never on my beat. It was the lowest per capita crime area in L.A. The University brass followed an implicit edict of letting rich black police rich black, as if they figured blue suits couldn't speak the language there at all. And the High Darktown citizens did a good job. Burglars foolish enough to trek across giant front lawns and punch in Tiffany windows were dispatched by volleys from thousand-dollar skeet guns held by negro financiers with an aristocratic panache to rival that of *anyone* white and big-moneyed. High Darktown did a damn good job of being inviolate.

But the legends were something else, and when I worked University, I wondered if they had been started and repeatedly embellished only because square-john white cops couldn't take the fact that there were "niggers," "shines," "spooks," and "jigs" who were capable of buying their low-rent lives outright. The stories ran from the relatively prosaic: negro bootleggers with mob connections taking their loot and buying liquor stores in Watts and wetback-staffed garment mills in San Pedro, to exotic: the same thugs flooding low darktowns with cut-rate heroin and pimping out their most beautiful high-yellow sweethearts to L.A.'s powers-that-be in order to circumvent licensing and real estate statutes enforcing racial exclusivity. There was only one common denominator to all the legends: it was agreed that although High Darktown money started out dirty, it was now squeaky clean and snow white.

Pulling up in front of the liquor store on Gramercy, I quickly scanned the dick's report on the robbery there, learning that the clerk was alone when it went down and saw both robbers up close before the white man pistol-whipped him unconscious. Wanting an eyeball witness to back up Lieutenant Holland's APB,

I entered the immaculate little shop and walked up to the counter.

A negro man with his head swathed in bandages walked in from the back. Eyeing me top to bottom, he said, "Yes, officer?"

I liked his brevity and reciprocated it. Holding up the mug shot of Wallace Simpkins, I said, "Is this one of the guys?"

Flinching backward, he said, "Yes. Get him."

"Bought and paid for," I said.

An hour later I had three more eyeball confirmations and turned my mind to strategy. With the all-points out on Simpkins, he'd probably get juked by the first blue suit who crossed his path, a thought only partly comforting. Artie Holland probably had stake-out teams stationed in the back rooms of other liquor stores in the area, and a prowl of Simpkins's known haunts was a ridiculous play for a solo white man. Parking on an elm-lined street, I watched Japanese gardeners tend football field–sized lawns and started to sense that Wild Wallace's affinity for High Dark-town and white partners was the lever I needed. I set out to trawl for pale-skinned intruders like myself.

South on La Brea to Jefferson, then up to Western and back over to Adams. Runs down 1st Avenue, 2nd Avenue, 3rd, 4th, and 5th. The only white men I saw were other cops, mailmen, store owners, and poontang prowlers. A circuit of the bars on Washington yielded no white faces and no known criminal types I could shake down for information.

Dusk found me hungry, angry, and still itchy, imagining Simpkins poking pins in a brand-new, plainclothes Blanchard doll. I stopped at a barbecue joint and wolfed down a beef sandwich, slaw, and fries. I was on my second cup of coffee when the mixed couple came in.

The girl was a pretty high yellow—soft angularity in a pink summer dress that tried to downplay her curves, and failed. The man was squat and muscular, wearing a rumpled Hawaiian shirt and pressed khaki trousers that looked like army issue. From my table I heard them place their order: jumbo chicken dinners for six with extra gravy and biscuits. "Lots of big appetites," the guy said to the counterman. When the line got him a deadpan, he goosed the girl with his knee. She moved away, clenching her fists and twisting her head as if trying to avoid an unwanted kiss. Catching her face full view, I saw loathing etched into every feature.

They registered as trouble, and I walked out to my car in order to tail them when they left the restaurant. Five minutes later they appeared, the girl walking ahead, the man a few paces behind her, tracing hourglass figures in the air and flicking his tongue like a lizard. They got into a prewar Packard sedan parked in front of me, Lizard Man taking the wheel. When they accelerated, I counted to ten and pursued.

The Packard was an easy surveillance. It had a long radio antenna topped with a foxtail, so I was able to remain several car lengths in back and use the tail as a sighting device. We moved out of High Darktown

215

on Western, and within minutes mansions and proudly tended homes were replaced by tenements and tar-paper shacks encircled by chicken wire. The farther south we drove the worse it got; when the Packard hung a left on 94th and headed east, past auto graveyards, storefront voodoo mosques and hair-straightening parlors, it felt like entering White Man's Hell.

At 94th and Normandie, the Packard pulled to the curb and parked; I continued on to the corner. From my rearview I watched Lizard Man and the girl cross the street and enter the only decent-looking house on the block, a whitewashed adobe job shaped like a miniature Alamo. Parking myself, I grabbed a flashlight from under the seat and walked over.

Right away I could tell the scene was way off. The block was nothing but welfare cribs, vacant lots, and gutted jalopies, but six beautiful '40–'41 vintage cars were stationed at curbside. Hunkering down, I flashed my light at their license plates, memorized the numbers, and ran back to my unmarked cruiser. Whispering hoarsely into the two-way, I gave R&I the figures and settled back to await the readout.

I got the kickback ten minutes later, and the scene went from way off to way, *way* off.

Cupping the radio mike to my ear and clamping my spare hand over it to hold the noise down, I took in the clerk's spiel. The Packard was registered to Leotis McCarver, male negro, age 41, of 1348 West 94th Street, L.A.—which had to be the cut-rate Alamo. His occupation was on file as union officer in the

Brotherhood of Sleeping Car Porters. The other vehicles were registered to negro and white thugs with strong-arm convictions dating back to 1922. When the clerk read off the last name—Ralph "Big Tuna" De Santis, a known Mickey Cohen trigger—I decided to give the Alamo a thorough crawling.

Armed with my flashlight and two pieces, I cut diagonally across vacant lots toward my target's back yard. In the far distance I could see fireworks lighting up the sky, but down here no one seemed to be celebrating—their war of just plain living was still dragging on. When I got to the Alamo's yard wall, I took it at a run and kneed and elbowed my way over the top, coming down onto soft grass.

The back of the house was dark and quiet, so I risked flashing my light. Seeing a service porch fronted by a flimsy wooden door, I tiptoed over and tried it—and found it unlocked.

I walked in flashlight first, my beam picking up dusty walls and floors, discarded lounge chairs, and a broom-closet door standing half open. Opening it all the way, I saw army officers' uniforms on hangers, replete with campaign ribbons and embroidered insignias.

Shouted voices jerked my attention toward the house proper. Straining my ears, I discerned both white- and negro-accented insults being hurled. There was a connecting door in front of me, with darkness beyond it. The shouting had to be issuing from a front room, so I nudged the door open a crack, then squatted down to listen as best I could.

"... and I'm just tellin' you we gots to find a place and get us off the streets," a negro voice was yelling, " 'cause even if we splits up, colored with colored and the whites with the whites, there is still gonna be roadblocks!"

A babble rose in response, then a shrill whistle silenced it, and a white voice dominated: "We'll be stopping the train way out in the country. Farmland. We'll destroy the signaling gear, and if the passengers take off looking for help, the nearest farmhouse is ten fucking miles away—and those dogfaces are gonna be on foot."

A black voice tittered, "They gonna be mad, them soldiers."

Another black voice: "They gonna fought the whole fucking war for free."

Laughter, then a powerful negro baritone took over: "Enough clowning around, this is money we're talking about and nothing else!"

" 'Cepting revenge, mister union big shot. Don't you forget I got me other business on that train."

I knew that voice by heart—it had voodoo-cursed my soul in court. I was on my way out the back for reinforcements when my legs went out from under me and I fell head first into darkness.

The darkness was soft and rippling, and I felt like I was swimming in a velvet ocean. Angry shouts reverberated far away, but I knew they were harmless; they were coming from another planet. Every so often I felt little stabs in my arms and saw pinpoints of light that made the voices louder, but then everything would go even softer, the velvet waves caressing me, smothering all my hurt.

Until the velvet turned to ice and the friendly little stabs became wrenching thuds up and down my back. I tried to draw myself into a ball, but an angry voice from this planet wouldn't let me. "Wake up, shitbird! We ain't wastin' no more pharmacy morph on you! Wake up! Wake up, goddamnit!"

Dimly I remembered that I was a police officer and went for the .38 on my hip. My arms and hands wouldn't move, and when I tried to lurch my whole body, I knew they were tied to my sides and that the thuds were kicks to my legs and rib cage. Trying to move away, I felt head-to-toe muscle cramps and opened my eyes. Walls and a ceiling came into hazy focus, and it all came back. I screamed something that was drowned out by laughter, and the Lizard Man's face hovered only inches above mine. "Lee Blanchard," he said, waving my badge and ID holder in front of my eyes. "You got sucker-punched again, shitbird. I saw Jimmy Bivins put you down at the Legion. Left hook outta nowhere, and you hit your knees, then worthless-shine muscle puts you down on your face. I got no respect for a man who gets sucker-punched by niggers."

At "niggers" I heard a gasp and twisted around to see the negro girl in the pink dress sitting in a chair a few feet away. Listening for background noises and hearing nothing, I knew the three of us were alone in the house. My eyes cleared a little more, and I saw that the velvet ocean was a plushly furnished living room. Feeling started to return to my limbs, sharp pain that cleared my fuzzy head. When I felt a grinding in my lower back, I winced; the extra .38 snub I had tucked into my waistband at City Hall was still there, slipped down into my skivvies. Reassured by it, I looked up at Lizard Face and said, "Robbed any liquor stores lately?"

He laughed. "A few. Chump change compared to the big one this after—"

The girl shrieked, "Don't tell him nothin'!"

Lizard Man flicked his tongue. "He's dead meat, so who cares? It's a train hijack, canvasback. Some army brass chartered the Super Chief, L.A. to Frisco. Poker games, hookers in the sleeping cars, smut movies in the lounge. Ain't you heard? The war's over, time to celebrate. We got hardware on board—shines playing porters, white guys in army suits. They all got scatterguns, and sweetie pie's boyfriend Voodoo, he's got himself a tommy. They're gonna take the train down tonight, around Salinas, when the brass is smashed to the gills, just achin' to throw away all that good separation pay. Then Voodoo's gonna come back here and perform some religious rites on you. He told me about it, said he's got this mean old pit bull named Revenge. A friend kept him while he was in Quentin. The buddy was white, and he tormented the dog so he hates white men worse than poison. The dog only gets fed about twice a week, and you can just bet he'd love a nice big bowl of canvasback stew. Which is you, white boy. Voodoo's gonna cut you up alive, turn you into dog food out of the can. Wanna take a bet on what he cuts off first?"

"That's not true! That's not what—"

"Shut up, Cora!"

Twisting on my side to see the girl better, I played a wild hunch. "Are you Cora Downey?"

Cora's jaw dropped, but Lizard spoke first. "Smart boy. Billy Boyle's ex, Voodoo's current. These high-yellow coozes get around. You know canvasback here, don't you, sweet? He sent both your boyfriends up, and if you're real nice, maybe Voodoo'll let you do some cutting on him."

Cora walked over and spat in my face. She hissed "Mother" and kicked me with a spiked toe. I tried to roll away, and she sent another kick at my back.

Then my ace in the hole hit me right between the eyes, harder than any of the blows I had absorbed so far. Last night I had heard Wallace Simpkins's voice through the door: " 'Cepting revenge, mister union big shot. I got me other business on that train." In my mind that "business" buzzed as snuffing Lieutenant Billy Boyle, and I was laying five-to-one that Cora wouldn't like the idea.

Lizard took Cora by the arm and led her to the couch, then squatted next to me. "You're a sucker for a spitball," he said.

I smiled up at him. "Your mother bats cleanup at a two-dollar whorehouse."

He slapped my face. I spat blood at him and said, "And you're ugly."

He slapped me again; when his arm followed

221

through I saw the handle of an automatic sticking out of his right pants pocket. I made my voice drip with contempt: "You hit like a girl. Cora could take you easy."

His next shot was full force. I sneered through bloody lips and said, "You queer? Only nancy boys slap like that."

A one-two set hit me in the jaw and neck, and I knew it was now or never. Slurring my words like a punch-drunk pug, I said, "Let me up. Let me up and I'll fight you man-to-man. Let me up."

Lizard took a penknife from his pocket and cut the rope that bound my arms to my sides. I tried to move my hands, but they were jelly. My battered legs had some feeling in them, so I rolled over and up onto my knees. Lizard had backed off into a chump's idea of a boxing stance and was firing roundhouse lefts and rights at the living room air. Cora was sitting on the couch, wiping angry tears from her cheeks. Deep breathing and lolling my torso like a hophead, I stalled for time, waiting for feeling to return to my hands.

"Get up, shitbird!"

My fingers still wouldn't move.

"I said get up!"

Still no movement.

Lizard came forward on the balls of his feet, feinting and shadowboxing. My wrists started to buzz with blood, and I began to get unprofessionally angry, like I was a rookie heavy, not a thirty-one-year-old cop. Lizard hit me twice, left, right, open-handed. In a split second he became Jimmy Bivins, and I zoomed back to the ninth round at the Legion in '37. Dropping my left shoulder, I sent out a right lead, then pulled it and left-hooked him to the breadbasket. Bivins gasped and bent forward; I stepped backward for swinging room. Then Bivins was Lizard going for his piece, and I snapped to where I really was.

We drew at the same time. Lizard's first shot went above my head, shattering a window behind me; mine, slowed by my awkward rear pull, slammed into the far wall. Recoil spun us both around, and before Lizard had time to aim I threw myself to the floor and rolled to the side like a carpet-eating dervish. Three shots cut the air where I had been standing a second before, and I extended my gun arm upward, braced my wrist, and emptied my snub-nose at Lizard's chest. He was blasted backward, and through the shots' echoes I heard Cora scream long and shrill.

I stumbled over to Lizard. He was on his way out, bleeding from three holes, unable to work the trigger of the .45. He got up the juice to give me a feeble middle-finger farewell, and when the bird was in mid-air I stepped on his heart and pushed down, squeezing the rest of his life out in a big arterial burst. When he finished twitching, I turned my attention to Cora, who was standing by the couch, putting out another shriek.

I stifled the noise by pinning her neck to the wall and hissing, "Questions and answers. Tell me what I want to know and you walk, fuck with me and I find dope in your purse and tell the DA you've been selling it to white nursery-school kids." I let up on my grip. "First question. Where's my car?"

Cora rubbed her neck. I could feel the obscenities stacking up on her tongue, itching to be hurled. All her rage went into her eyes as she said, "Out back. The garage."

"Have Simpkins and the stiff been clouting the liquor stores in West Adams?"

Cora stared at the floor and nodded, "Yes." Looking up, here eyes were filled with the self-disgust of the freshly turned stoolie. I said, "McCarver the union guy thought up the train heist?"

Another affirmative nod.

Deciding not to mention Billy Boyle's probable presence on the train, I said, "Who's bankrolling? Buying the guns and uniforms?"

"The liquor store money was for that, and there was this rich guy fronting money."

Now the big question. "When does the train leave Union Station?"

Cora looked at her watch. "In half an hour."

I found a phone in the hallway and called the Central Division squadroom, telling Georgie Caulkins to send all his available plainclothes and uniformed officers to Union Station, that an army-chartered Super Chief about to leave for 'Frisco was going to be hit by a white–negro gang in army and porter outfits. Lowering my voice so Cora wouldn't hear, I told him to detain a negro quartermaster lieutenant named William Boyle as a material witness, then hung up before he could say anything but "Jesus Christ."

Cora was smoking a cigarette when I reentered the living room. I picked my badge holder up off the floor and heard sirens approaching. "Come on," I said. "You don't want to get stuck here when the bulls show up."

Cora flipped her cigarette at the stiff, then kicked him one for good measure. We took off.

I ran code three all the way downtown. Adrenaline smothered the dregs of the morph still in my system, and anger held down the lid on the aches all over my body. Cora sat as far away from me as she could without hanging out the window and never blinked at the siren noise. I started to like her and decided to doctor my arresting officer's report to keep her out of the shithouse.

Nearing Union Station, I said, "Want to sulk or want to survive?"

Cora spat out the window and balled her fists.

"Want to get skin searched by some dyke matrons over at city jail or you want to go home?"

Cora's fist balls tightened up; the knuckles were as white as my skin.

"Want Voodoo to snuff Billy Boyle?"

That got her attention. "What!"

I looked sidelong at Cora's face gone pale. "He's on the train. You think about that when we get to the station and a lot of cops start asking you to snitch off your pals."

Pulling herself in from the window, Cora asked me the question that hoods have been asking cops since they patrolled on dinosaurs: "Why you do this shitty kind of work?"

I ignored it and said, "Snitch. It's in your best interest."

"That's for me to decide. Tell me."

"Tell you what?"

"Why you do—"

I interrupted, "You've got it all figured out, you tell me."

Cora started ticking off points on her fingers, leaning toward me so I could hear her over the siren. "One, you yourself figured your boxin' days would be over when you was thirty, so you got yourself a nice civil service pension job; two, the bigwig cops loves to have ball players and fighters around to suck up to them—so's you gets the first crack at the cushy 'signments. Three, you likes to hit people, and *po*-lice work be full of that; four, your ID card said Warrants Division, and I knows that warrants cops all serves process and does repos on the side, so I knows you pickin' up lots of extra change. Five—"

I held up my hands in mock surrender, feeling like I had just taken four hard jabs from Billy Conn and didn't want to go for sloppy fifths. "Smart girl, but you forgot to mention that I work goon squad for Firestone Tire and get a kickback for fingering wetbacks to the Border Patrol."

Cora straightened the knot in my disreputable necktie. "Hey, baby, a gig's a gig, you gots to take it where you finds it. I done things I ain't particularly proud of, and I—"

I shouted, "That's not it!"

Cora moved back to the window and smiled. "It certainly is, Mr. Po-liceman."

Angry now, angry at losing, I did what I always did when I smelled defeat: attack. "Shitcan it. Shitcan it now, before I forget I was starting to like you."

Cora gripped the dashboard with two white-knuckled hands and stared through the windshield. Union Station came into view, and pulling into the parking lot I saw a dozen black-and-whites and un-marked cruisers near the front entrance. Bullhorn-barked commands echoed unintelligibly as I killed my siren, and behind the police cars I glimpsed plain-clothesmen aiming riot guns at the ground.

I pinned my badge to my jacket front and said, "Out." Cora stumbled from the car and stood rubber-kneed on the pavement. I got out, grabbed her arm, and shoved-pulled her all the way over to the pande-monium. As we approached, a harness bull leveled his .38 at us, then hesitated and said, "Sergeant Blanchard?"

I said "Yeah" and handed Cora over to him, add-ing, "She's a material witness, be nice to her." The youth nodded, and I walked past two bumper-to-bumper black-and-whites into the most incredible shakedown scene I had ever witnessed:

Negro men in porter uniforms and white men in army khakis were lying facedown on the pavement, their jackets and shirts pulled up to their shoulders, their trousers and undershorts pulled down to their knees. Uniformed cops were spread searching them while plainclothesmen held the muzzles of .12 gauge pumps to their heads. A pile of confiscated pistols and sawed-off shotguns lay a safe distance away. The men on the ground were all babbling their innocence or shouting epithets, and every cop trigger finger looked itchy.

Voodoo Simpkins and Billy Boyle were not among the six suspects. I looked around for familiar cop faces and saw Georgie Caulkins by the station's front entrance, standing over a sheet-covered stretcher. I ran up to him and said, "What have you got, Skipper?"

Caulkins toed the sheet aside, revealing the remains of a fortyish negro man. "The shine's Leotis Mc-Carver," Georgie said. "Upstanding colored citizen, Brotherhood of Sleeping Car Porters big shot, a credit to his race. Put a .38 to his head and blew his brains out when the black-and-whites showed up."

Catching a twinkle in the old lieutenant's eyes, I said, "Really?"

Georgie smiled. "I can't shit a shitter. McCarver came out waving a white handkerchief, and some punk kid rookie cancelled his ticket. Deserves a commendation, don't you think?"

I looked down at the stiff and saw that the entry wound was right between the eyes. "Give him a sharpshooter's medal and a desk job before he plugs some innocent civilian. What about Simpkins and Boyle?"

"Gone," Georgie said. "When we first got here, we didn't know the real soldiers and porters from the heisters, so we threw a net over the whole place and shook everybody down. We held every legit shine lieutenant, which was two guys, then cut them loose when they weren't your boy. Simpkins and Boyle probably got away in the shuffle. A car got stolen from the other end of the lot—citizen said she saw a nigger in a porter's suit breaking the window. That was probably Simpkins. The license number's on the air along with an all points. That shine is dead meat."

I thought of Simpkins invoking protective voodoo gods and said, "I'm going after him myself."

"You owe me a report on this thing!"

"Later."

"Now!"

I said, "Later, sir," and ran back to Cora, Georgie's "now" echoing behind me. When I got to where I had left her, she was gone. Looking around, I saw her a few yards away on her knees, handcuffed to the bumper of a black-and-white. A cluster of blue suits were hooting at her, and I got very angry.

I walked over. A particularly callow-looking rookie was regaling the others with his account of Leotis Mc-Carver's demise. All four snapped to when they saw me coming. I grabbed the storyteller by his necktie and yanked him toward the back of the car. "Uncuff her," I said.

The rookie tried to pull away. I yanked at his tie until we were face-to-face and I could smell Sen-Sen on his breath. "And apologize."

The kid flushed, and I walked back to my unmarked cruiser. I heard muttering behind me, and then I felt a tap on my shoulder. Cora was there, smiling. "I owe you one," she said.

I pointed to the passenger seat. "Get in. I'm collecting."

The ride back to West Adams was fueled by equal parts of my nervous energy and Cora's nonstop spiel on her loves and criminal escapades. I had seen it dozens of times before. A cop stands up for a prisoner against another cop, on general principles or because the other cop is a turd, and the prisoner takes it as a sign of affection and respect and proceeds to lay out a road map of their life, justifying every wrong turn because he wants to be the cop's moral equal. Cora's tale of her love for Billy Boyle back in his heister days, her slide into call-house service when he went to prison, and her lingering crush on Wallace Simpkins was predictable and mawkishly rendered. I got more and more embarrassed by her "you dig?" punctuations and taps on the arm, and if I didn't need her as a High Darktown tour guide I would have kicked her out of the car and back to her old life. But then the monologue got interesting.

When Billy Boyle was cut loose from Chino, he had a free week in L.A. before his army induction and went looking for Cora. He found her hooked on ether at Minnie Roberts's Casbah, seeing voodoo visions, servicing customers as Coroloa, the African Slave Queen. He got her out of there, eased her off the dope with steambaths and vitamin B-12 shots, then ditched her to fight for Uncle Sam. Something snapped in her brain when Billy left, and, still vamped on Wallace Simpkins, she started writing him at Quentin. Knowing his affinity for voodoo, she smuggled in some slave-queen smut pictures taken of her at the Casbah, and they got a juicy correspondence going. Meanwhile, Cora went to work at Mickey Cohen's southside numbers mill, and everything looked peachy. Then Simpkins came out of Big Q, the voodoo sex fantasy stuff became tepid reality, and the Voodoo Man himself went back to stickups, exploiting her connections to the white criminal world.

When Cora finished her story, we were skirting the edge of High Darktown. It was dusk; the temperature was easing off; the neon signs of the Western Avenue juke joints had just started flashing. Cora lit a cigarette and said, "All Billy's people is from around here. If he's lookin' for a hideout or a travelin' stake, he'd hit the clubs on West Jeff. Wallace wouldn't show his evil face around here, 'less he's lookin' for Billy, which I figure he undoubtedly is. I—"

I interrupted, "I thought Billy came from a square-john family. Wouldn't he go to them?"

Cora's look said I was a lily-white fool. "Ain't no square-john families around here, 'ceptin those who work domestic. West Adams was built on bootlegging, sweetie. Black sellin' white lightnin' to black, gettin' fat, then investin' white. Billy's folks was runnin' shine when I was in pigtails. They're respectable now, and they hates him for takin' a jolt. He'll be callin' in favors at the clubs, don't you worry."

I hung a left on Western, heading for Jefferson Boulevard. "How do you know all this?"

"I am from High, *High* Darktown, sweet."

"Then why do you hold on to that Aunt Jemima accent?"

Cora laughed. "And I thought I sounded like Lena Horne. Here's why, sweetcakes. Black woman with a law degree they call 'nigger.' Black girl with three-inch heels and a shiv in her purse they call 'baby.' You dig?"

"I dig."

"No, you don't. Stop the car, Tommy Tucker's club is on the next block."

I said, "Yes, ma'am," and pulled to the curb. Cora got out ahead of me and swayed around the corner on her three-inch heels, calling, "I'll go in," over her shoulder. I waited underneath a purple neon sign heralding "Tommy Tucker's Playroom." Cora come out five minutes later, saying, "Billy was in here 'bout half an hour ago. Touched the barman for a double saw."

"Simpkins?"

Cora shook her head. "Ain't been seen."

I hooked a finger in the direction of the car. "Let's catch him."

For the next two hours we followed Billy Boyle's trail through High Darktown's nightspots. Cora went in and got the information, while I stood outside like a white wallflower, my gun unholstered and pressed to my leg, waiting for a voodoo killer with a tommy gun to aim and fire. Her info was always the same: Boyle had been in, had made a quick impression with his army threads, had gotten a quick touch based on his rep, and had practically run out the door. And no one had seen Wallace Simpkins.

11 P.M. found me standing under the awning of Hanks' Swank Spot, feeling pinpricks all over my exhausted body. Square-john negro kids cruised by waving little American flags out of backseat windows, still hopped up that the war was over. Male and female, they all had mug-shot faces that kept my trigger finger at half-pull even though I knew damn well they couldn't be *him*. Cora's sojourn inside was running three times as long as her previous ones, and when a car backfired and I aimed at the old lady behind the wheel, I figured High Darktown was safer with me off the street and went in to see what was keeping Cora.

The Swank Spot's interior was Egyptian: silk wallpaper embossed with pharaohs and mummies, papermache pyramids surrounding the dance floor, and a long bar shaped like a crypt lying sideways. The patrons were more contemporary: negro men in double-breasted suits and women in evening gowns who looked disapprovingly at my rumpled clothes and two-and-a-half-day beard.

Ignoring them, I eyeballed in vain for Cora. Her soiled pink dress would have stood out like a beacon amid the surrounding hauteur, but all the women were dressed in pale white and sequined black. Panic was rising inside me when I heard her voice, distorted by bebop, pleading behind the dance floor.

I pushed my way through minglers, dancers, and three pyramids to get to her. She was standing next to a phonograph setup, gesturing at a black man in slacks and a camel-hair jacket. The man was sitting in a folding chair, alternately admiring his manicure and looking at Cora like she was dirt.

The music was reaching a crescendo; the man smiled at me; Cora's pleas were engulfed by saxes, horns, and drums going wild. I flashed back to my Legion days—rabbit punches and elbows and scrubbing my laces into cuts during clinches. The past two days went topsy-turvy, and I kicked over the phonograph. The Benny Goodman sextet exploded into silence, and I aimed my piece at the man and said, *"Tell me now."*

Shouts rose from the dance floor, and Cora pressed herself into a toppled pyramid. The man smoothed the pleats in his trousers and said, "Cora's old flame was in about half an hour ago, begging. I turned him down, because I respect my origins and hate snitches. But I told him about an old mutual friend—a soft touch. Another Cora flame was in about ten minutes ago, asking after flame number one. Seems he has a grudge against him. I sent him the same place."

I croaked, "Where?" and my voice sounded disembodied to my own ears. The man said, "No. You can apologize now, officer. Do it, and I won't tell my good friends Mickey Cohen and Inspector Waters about your behavior."

I stuck my gun in my waistband and pulled out an old Zippo I used to light suspects' cigarettes. Sparking a flame, I held it inches from a stack of brocade curtains. "Remember the Coconut Grove?"

The man said, "You wouldn't," and I touched the flame to the fabric. It ignited immediately, and smoke rose to the ceiling. Patrons were screaming "Fire!" in the club proper. The brocade was fried to a crisp when the man shrieked, "John Downey," ripped off his camel hair and flung it at the flames. I grabbed Cora and pulled her through the club, elbowing and rabbit punching panicky revelers to clear a path. When we hit the sidewalk, I saw that Cora was sobbing. Smoothing her hair, I whispered hoarsely, "What, babe, what?"

It took a moment for Cora to find a voice, but when she spoke, she sounded like a college professor. "John Downey's my father. He's very big around here, and he hates Billy because he thinks Billy made me a whore."

"Where does he li—"

"Arlington and Country Club."

We were there within five minutes. This was High, *High* Darktown—Tudor estates, French chateaus, and Moorish villas with terraced front lawns. Cora pointed out a plantation-style mansion and said, "Go to the side door. Thursday's the maid's night off, and nobody'll hear you if you knock at the front."

I stopped the car across the street and looked for other out-of-place vehicles. Seeing nothing but Packards, Caddys, and Lincolns nestled in driveways, I said, "Stay put. Don't move, no matter what you see or hear."

Cora nodded mutely. I got out and ran over to the plantation, hurdling a low iron fence guarded by a

white iron jockey, then treading down a long driveway. Laughter and applause issued from the adjoining
mansion, separated from the Downey place by a high
hedgerow. The happy sounds covered my approach,
and I started looking in windows.

Standing on my toes and moving slowly toward the
back of the house, I saw rooms festooned with crewel-
work wall hangings and hunting prints. Holding my
face up to within a few inches of the glass, I looked
for shadow movement and listened for voices, wondering why all the lights were on at close to midnight.

Then faceless voices assailed me from the next window down. Pressing my back to the wall, I saw that
the window was cracked for air. Cocking an ear toward
the open space, I listened.

". . . and after all the setup money I put in, you
still had to knock down those liquor stores?"

The tone reminded me of a mildly outraged negro
minister rebuking his flock, and I braced myself for
the voice that I knew would reply.

"I gots cowboy blood, Mister Downey, like you
musta had when you was a young man runnin' shine.
That cop musta got loose, got Cora and Whitey to
snitch. Blew a sweet piece of work, but we can still
get off clean. McCarver was the only one 'sides me
knew you was bankrollin', and he be dead. Billy be
the one *you* wants dead, and he be showin' up soon.
Then I cuts him and dumps him somewhere, and nobody knows he was even here."

"You want money, don't you?"

"Five big get me lost somewheres nice, then maybe

when he starts feelin' safe again, I comes back and cuts that cop. That sound about—"

Applause from the big house next door cut Simpkins off. I pulled out my piece and got up some guts, knowing my only safe bet was to backshoot the son of a bitch right where he was. I heard more clapping and joyous shouts that Mayor Bowron's reign was over, and then John Downey's preacher baritone was back in force: "I want him dead. My daughter is a white-trash consort and a whore, and he's—"

A scream went off behind me, and I hit the ground just as machine-gun fire blew the window to bits. Another burst took out the hedgerow and the next-door window. I pinned myself back first to the wall and drew myself upright as the snout of a tommy gun was rested against the ledge a few inches away. When muzzle flame and another volley exploded from it, I stuck my .38 in blind and fired six times at stomach level. The tommy strafed a reflex burst upward, and when I hit the ground again, the only sound was chaotic shrieks from the other house.

I reloaded from a crouch, then stood up and surveyed the carnage through both mansion windows. Wallace Simpkins lay dead on John Downey's Persian carpet, and across the way I saw a banner for the West Adams Democratic Club streaked with blood. When I saw a dead woman spread-eagled on top of an antique table, I screamed myself, elbowed my way into Downey's den, and picked up the machine gun. The grips burned my hands, but I didn't care; I saw the faces of every boxer who had ever defeated me and didn't care; I heard grenades going off in my brain and was glad they were there to kill all the innocent screaming. With the tommy's muzzle as my directional device, I walked through the house.

All my senses went into my eyes and trigger finger. Wind ruffled a window curtain, and I blew the wall apart; I caught my own image in a gilt-edged mirror and blasted myself into glass shrapnel. Then I heard a woman moaning, "Daddy, Daddy, Daddy," dropped the tommy, and ran to her.

Cora was on her knees on the entry hall floor, plunging a shiv into a man who had to be her father. The man moaned baritone low and tried to reach up, almost as if to embrace her. Cora's "Daddy's" got lower and lower, until the two seemed to be working toward harmony. When she let the dying man hold her, I gave them a moment together, then pulled Cora off of him and dragged her outside. She went limp in my arms, and with lights going on everywhere and sirens converging from all directions, I carried her to my car.

Some Jobs Are Simple

CHET WILLIAMSON

Chet Williamson's stories have appeared in Play-
boy, New Yorker, Magazine of Fantasy and Science Fiction, Twilight Zone, Games, *and* Alfred
Hitchcock's Mystery Magazine, *where his "Season
Pass," an Edgar nominee, was published. Two
novels,* The Pines *and* Ash Wednesday, *are forth-
coming from Tor Books. A third,* Only Business,
*is under revision, and he is currently writing his
fourth book, a novel about a small-city detective,*
McKain's Dilemma.

*Though Williamson has written few mysteries
to date, his long interest in Hammett, Chandler,
and the* Black Mask *writers, as well as his delight
in such contemporary authors as Elmore Leonard
and Robert B. Parker, have led him to the genre.*

*Williamson, 37, is a full-time free-lancer and
lives with his wife and son amid ever-growing piles
of books. He has no idea whatever of where "Some
Jobs Are Simple" came from, other than from his
typewriter. "Sometimes they're just there. I think
people sneak in at night and leave them."*

"IT TOOK ME a long time to find you," she
said, looking across the beer-wet table at
him. She was a hassled-looking woman, he thought as
he looked back and sipped his drink. Young, but not
so young that she could hide those bags under her
eyes with makeup.

"You sure I'm who you're looking for?"

"If your name's Joe, you are."

He nodded. "Joe."

"I need a . . . something done."

"A job."

"Yes. A job."

"Who told you about me?"

"An acquaintance. He owns . . . owned a fur-storage place."

"Uh-huh." Abrams, he thought. He'd torched the building six months before.

"Not him really. His wife."

"What's the job?"

She looked around nervously. "Can we talk here?"

"See any cops?"

She started to answer before she realized he was joking.

"Don't be so nervous," he said with a thin smile. "You, uh . . ." He glanced down, then up. "You want me to *do* somebody for you?"

"No!" Her eyelids flew up. "Oh no, nothing like that."

"What then?"

"A burglary." She had trouble with the word. It seemed to stick in her throat. He gestured to the half pitcher of beer, but she shook her head. "I want you to burglarize my house. Steal some jewelry of mine."

"Steal your own jewelry. That means insurance."

"Yes. I need money."

"And I give you back the jewels afterwards."

"Well, yes."

"And you pay me."

"Yes."

"You pay me a thousand dollars."

"A . . . that's more than I had thought."

"I'm taking a risk. You see? Any less and it's not worth it."

"A thousand dollars."

"I generally ask for more. Things are slow right now."

"You'd want cash."

He chuckled softly. "Yes indeed."

"Oh!" She looked embarrassed. "Yes. Yes, of course."

"Where do you live?"

"Marion Court. 1636 Marion Court."

He licked the beer from his lip. Marion Court was an upper-class section on the city's outskirts. The houses were widely spaced. "Who else lives there?"

"Just my husband."

"He in on this?"

"He . . . no, he's not. I don't want him to know about it."

"He'll know when the jewels are gone."

"I mean about my meeting you."

"Why not?"

"I need the money for something I don't want him to know about."

"Uh-huh."

"And that's all I want to say about it."

He poured himself more beer and took a swallow. "Once I steal the jewels, how do you know I'll give them back?"

"I would have to trust you."

"I'm a thief."

"If you kept them," she frowned, "I could tell the police you took them."

"Then I'd tell that you hired me to take them."

"You couldn't prove that."

"Then how else would you know that I took them?" A cloud passed over her face, and she moved back, as if trying to decide whether or not to rise from the table. "Don't worry," he said. "You'll get them back. I didn't get my reputation by double-crossing clients. I just want you to know that if you change your mind and get religion, I can take you with me, okay?"

"I won't change my mind."

"Good. When do you want this done?"

"Tomorrow night?"

"That's pretty soon." She didn't respond. "Okay. What time?"

"Two A.M.? You can come in through the kitchen door. I'll have it unlocked. I'll put the jewelry on the desk in the den. It's just off the kitchen."

"Won't your husband think that's odd?"

"He never goes into the den after dinner. When you leave, break the window in the kitchen door."

"Why?"

She beamed as if she were proud of her idea. "That way it won't look as though it was unlocked to begin with."

"Clever. Won't your husband hear it?"

"He's a sound sleeper, and our bedroom's upstairs on the other side of the house."

"Does he have a gun?"

"A gun? Yes. Why?"

"There's always a chance he'll wake up. A chance he'll hear me. Which means I've got to bring a gun."

"No! You won't need it—he'll never hear you, and if he does I'll keep him in the bedroom."

"I'm sorry, but . . ."

"Please, I promise you, you won't need a gun. I'll . . . I'll unload his."

"Bringing it doesn't mean I have to use it."

"I . . ."

"Insurance, that's all. If you know I've got a gun, you'll be doubly sure I won't be bothered."

She sat for a moment, looking worried. "All right. But please, no shooting."

"No shooting. Any pets?"

"No. How can I reach you afterward?"

He scribbled a number on a corner of the paper place mat, tore it off, and handed it to her. "Call this number. If I'm not there, there'll be someone who'll tell you how to reach me. Memorize it and throw it away."

She nodded and stuck the note in her purse. "1636 Marion Court. Two A.M. You won't forget?"

"I won't forget."

The following night he parked his car, a dark blue midsized sedan, four blocks from 1636 Marion and walked to the house. He was relieved to see that it was a good fifty yards between houses and relieved to hear no bayings of dogs as he walked up the driveway and around to the kitchen door. He slipped on his gloves and tried the knob. It was unlocked, as she'd promised, and opened smoothly and quietly. He listened, but the house was still. Closing the door behind him, he took a penlight from his pocket and flashed it low around the room, quickly spotting the entrance to the den. The door was open, and on the desk was a brown leather box. He opened the lid and smiled as the jewelry danced in the light. It was always tempting, but he'd never yet succumbed. With this batch, though, it would be hard, very hard.

His head shot up as he heard the noise, a low squeak, as of a settling floorboard. But he knew the difference between a settling sound and one made by someone's foot. He flicked off the penlight and reached for the .38 Special in his armpit.

"Hello?" The voice was a whisper, high and near. "Is that you . . . Joe?" She said the name as though she knew it was false.

He held the light out at his side and turned it on. She was standing empty-handed in the doorway, a cranberry-colored robe wrapped around her. She blinked as the light hit her eyes. "Jesus," he said. "What are you doing here?"

"I was nervous. I couldn't stay in bed. I wanted to make sure you got in all right."

"Of course I did. I thought you were going to stay with your husband."

"Oh, he's sleeping, don't worry." She pointed to the box. "Those are the jewels."

"I figured."

"And there was another piece I wore today that I forgot to put in the box . . ." Her hand went into the pocket of her robe and came out with a small pistol that fired twice, throwing bullets sharply into his chest so that he staggered back and hit the wall of bookcases, dropping his own pistol he'd been loosely, confidently holding. He slumped to the floor, books plopping on either side of him like giant raindrops. He didn't have to see the blood to know he was dying.

With the same surprising speed with which she'd drawn the gun, she crossed to him from the doorway, knelt, and picked up his .38. He tried to make a grab for it, but only his fingers would move, and those too slowly. "Why?" he asked, tasting blood.

"You'll see. You deserve that much." She crossed to the doorway, turned on the room light, and shouted. "Tom!" There was silence. "*Tom!*" She wrapped a handkerchief around the hand that held the gun.

A muffled cry answered her from somewhere in the house.

"Come here!" I'm in the den!"

"What is it? For crissake, it's after two . . ."

"Just come in here! Something's not right . . ." She walked over to where he'd been standing when she'd shot him and looked at him. "Now you get it?"

A few seconds later Tom walked through the doorway, and she shot him in the forehead with the .38. Then she wiped the other pistol and put it in her husband's dead hand. "You'll get yours back in a minute," she said to the man dying against the bookcase. "I've got a couple of things to do first."

He listened to her call the police on the kitchen phone, thinking how frenzied and horrified she seemed. The last sound he heard was the sharp clatter of glass as she broke the window in the kitchen door. From the outside, of course.

Subscription to THE NEW BLACK MASK
$27.80/year in the U.S.

Subscription correspondence should be sent to
THE NEW BLACK MASK
129 West 56th Street
New York, NY 10019